Ans	_____	M.L.	_____
ASH	_____	MLW	_____
Bev	_____	Mt.Pl	_____
C.C.	_____	NLM	_____
C.P.	_____	Ott	_____
Dick	_____	PC	_____
DRZ	_____	PH	_____
ECH	_____	P.P.	_03/09_
ECS	_____	Pion.P.	_____
Gar	_____	Q.A.	_____
GRM	_9/09(wАи)_	Riv	_____
GSP	_____	RPP	_____
G.V.	_____	Ross	_____
Har	_____	S.C.	_____
JPCP	_____	St.A.	_____
KEN	_____	St.J	_____
K.L.	_02/10_	St.Joa	_____
K.M.	_____	St.M.	_____
L.H.	_____	Sgt	_7/07(Sнои)_
LO	_____	T.H.	_____
Lyn	_____	TLLO	_____
L.V.	_4/08_	T.M.	_____
McC	_____	T.T.	_____
McG	_____	Ven	_____
McQ	_____	Vets	_____
MIL	_____	VP	_____
	_____	Wat	_____
	_____	Wed	_____
	_____	WIL	_____
	_____	W.L.	_____

Melinda Hammond lives in a farmhouse on the edge of the Pennines. Her interests include theatre and music, and supporting her son's go-kart racing team — although she feels obliged to stay at home and keep the log fire burning during the winter months.

Visit the author's website at
http://myweb.tiscali.co.uk/melham

GENTLEMEN IN QUESTION

In the closing months of 1792, the terror of the French Revolution forces Camille, the young Comte du Vivière, to flee his homeland and seek refuge with his relatives in England. For Madeleine, the arrival of her handsome French cousin marks a change in her so far uneventful existence, and soon she finds herself caught up in a dangerous web of intrigue that also entangles Camille. But is he victim or villain?

Books by Melinda Hammond
Published by The House of Ulverscroft:

SUMMER CHARADE
FORTUNE'S LADY
AUTUMN BRIDE
THE HIGHCLOUGH LADY
A LADY AT MIDNIGHT
DANCE FOR A DIAMOND

MELINDA HAMMOND

GENTLEMEN IN QUESTION

Complete and Unabridged

ULVERSCROFT
Leicester

First published in Great Britain in 2006 by
Robert Hale Limited
London

First Large Print Edition
published 2007
by arrangement with
Robert Hale Limited
London

British Library CIP Data

Hammond, Melinda
  Gentlemen in question.—Large print ed.—
  Ulverscroft large print series: historical romance
  1. France—History—Revolution, *1789 – 1799*—Refugees
  —Fiction 2. Great Britain—History—George III,
  1760 – 1820—Fiction 3. Love stories 4. Large type books
  I. Title
  823.9'14 [F]

  ISBN 978–1–84617–782–8

Published by
F. A. Thorpe (Publishing)
Anstey, Leicestershire

Set by Words & Graphics Ltd.
Anstey, Leicestershire
Printed and bound in Great Britain by
T. J. International Ltd., Padstow, Cornwall

This book is printed on acid-free paper

1

The November day had begun bright and sunny, but now as the afternoon wore on, grey clouds were gathering ominously over the busy port of Rye. In a private parlour at the Three Barrels, a large gentleman in a brown bag-wig stood by the window looking out at the darkening sky. The elder of the two ladies seated by a crackling fire addressed him.

'It was fine enough when we arrived, sir. Surely the boat will come soon.'

Mr Sedgewick shook his head at his wife.

'I don't know, my dear, for I'm no sailor. Who can say if the French coast was stormy this morning?'

'Oh it seems cruel that poor Camille should have to suffer so much!' cried Mrs Sedgewick. 'What with his father dying so young, and it is but a year ago the poor young man lost his mother. And now those villains who claim to be the representatives of the people have robbed him of his estates and he is fleeing from the country he has always called home.'

'Well let us hope the *comte* is a good

sailor,' remarked the young lady sitting beside her. 'If not he will have sea-sickness to add to his woes.'

'Madeleine, how can you be so insensitive!'

Miss Sedgewick immediately begged pardon.

'I joke because I am uneasy, Mama, you know that,' she said contritely. 'And I worry how Grandpapa will receive Camille. You know he never forgave my aunt for marrying the Comte du Vivière. He is sure to have something cutting to say to their son.'

The door of the room opened and three anxious faces turned towards the landlord, who entered bearing a tray.

'No news yet, sir, I'm sorry,' he said cheerfully, 'but don't you worry now, my Ted's a bright lad, he'll run back here as soon as the packet comes into view.'

'*If* it comes,' put in the gentleman gloomily.

'Aye, well, there is that,' returned their host diffidently. 'They Frenchies is a funny lot, y'know, and with so much unrest in the country, mayhap they won't accommodate English vessels just now, although we've had no trouble as yet.'

'Oh I cannot even consider such a thing!' cried Mrs Sedgewick, 'How I wish there were some way of knowing what is happening.'

'Don't you go fretting yourself, ma'am. I was only surmising, after all. I'm sure everything's going along just fine — why, the packet's often late at this time o'year. The Channel can be very stormy, y'know.' The landlord did his best to reassure her. 'Now, I have brought you some coffee and a cheese pie, and I'll wager that by the time you have finished that, there'll be some news for you. After all, the sea's as unpredictable as a woman — beggin' your pardon, ladies — she don't follow any rules of man's making.'

'He seems a very sensible man,' remarked Miss Sedgewick as the landlord withdrew. 'No doubt he has a great deal of experience in these matters. Mama, pray do not look so anxious! Come, I will pour you a little coffee. That will make you feel better. And for you, Papa?'

'Thank you.'

Mr Sedgewick came away from the window to take the cup she held out for him and, meeting her troubled gaze, he smiled down at her.

'What, Maddie, are you anxious, too? I had come to believe you had no nerves.'

She smiled.

'Grandpapa says I have inherited his spirit, does he not? I only pray I do *not* have his bad temper! However, in this instance I must own I am a little apprehensive. One hears such horrific tales from those poor people who have already escaped from France. And we have only received the one letter from Camille. What if he has been arrested, and thrown into prison like so many of his compatriots?'

Mr Sedgewick patted her cheek reassuringly.

'Do not forget that when the *comte* wrote to us, he assured us that his cousin, the lawyer in Paris, had obtained the necessary papers for him to leave the country. He was confident there would be no problem.'

'Yes, I keep telling myself that, and yet I cannot be easy.'

There was a knock at the door and the landlord appeared, beaming broadly.

'My lad's come in this very minute sir, and tells me the packet's in view now.'

'Thank you, Sacher.'

Mr Sedgewick snatched up his greatcoat and shrugged himself into it while the ladies threw on their own travelling cloaks and made ready to accompany him to the quayside.

'Shall I order a carriage sir?'

'Thank you, Sacher, but no,' declared Mr Sedgewick, pleased to be moving at last. 'It's but a short step to the quay — it will be as quick to walk as to wait for the coach.'

He led the way out of the inn, setting a

brisk pace for the ladies who followed him. Their quickest way led through the Strand with its maze of wooden buildings, warehouses and stores for the shippers who used the harbour regularly. The sun had finally vanished behind the heavy clouds and they found themselves moving through a grey twilight. Miss Sedgewick thought she could hear sounds of activity ahead, carried towards them on the freshening breeze. By mischance a sudden gust of wind sent her heavy cloak billowing. She felt a tug as her gown became caught upon some obstacle. Halting, Madeleine saw that the edge of her open robe had become ensnared upon a splinter of wood protruding from one of the timber buildings. Curbing her impatience, she resisted the impulse to pull the gown and carefully eased the material free. It had taken only a moment, but when she looked up her parents had disappeared around the corner, obviously unaware of her plight. She was not unduly worried, for they had walked that route at least three times that day and she knew her way. Holding her cloak firmly she hurried on, taking no notice of two burly individuals approaching. As the men drew nearer, they crossed in front of her, and one of them addressed her in a rough, loud voice.

'And where might ye be off to in sich a

hurry, me beauty?'

'Excuse me.' She tried to move on but they blocked her way.

'Have ye no kind words for a brave sailor, then?'

'Please, let me pass.' Madeleine spoke calmly, but as she moved to one side she felt a hand steal round her waist and she dealt its owner a ringing slap across his cheek.

'Oh ho!' he laughed, 'Too good for the likes of us, are you, me lady!'

'How dare you! Let me go at once!'

She was unable to free herself from his iron grasp and for a moment she feared she might faint as the sailor pressed close to her, his malodorous breath hot on her face.

Then, miraculously, she was free. The sudden release surprised her into losing her balance and she fell to the ground. Looking up, she was in time to see one of her attackers crash to the floor and stay there, nursing a bloody nose, while the other grappled with a tall, powerful-looking figure. The conflict was over in an instant, the newcomer giving his opponent a violent blow to the body that made him stagger and the two assailants, seeing their opponent advancing upon them once more, gave up the struggle and took to their heels.

Miss Sedgewick had by this time risen to

her feet and she regarded her champion as he approached her, dusting his hands together. His appearance struck her as unusual, although she could not think why that should be. He was shabbily dressed in loose pantaloons with a sleeveless carmagnole jacket over a grubby white shirt, the sleeves of which were rolled up to display his powerful arms. His dark hair had escaped from its cord and hung loose and dishevelled to his shoulders, a shade darker than the bushy beard that covered most of his face; yet, despite his rough looks, he carried himself with an air of assurance, a man used to command. A military man, perhaps . . . she realized he was watching her, a faint look of amusement in his deep-blue eyes.

'Well, m'lady, you've taken no hurt, I trust?' His voice was deep with a north-country accent.

'No, thanks to your timely intervention.' Her eyes fell to his shirt which had been torn open in the scuffle to disclose an ugly red gash across the right side of his neck, 'But you are injured.'

He laughed, putting his hand up to the mark.

'Nay, lady, I gained this in t'service of my country.'

A second glance showed Madeleine that

the cut was partially healed, but his words gave her thoughts another turn.

'You are a sailor, perhaps?'

'Aye, something in that line, my lady.'

'The life of a seafaring man cannot be a prosperous one,' she said, pulling a stocking purse from her pocket and holding it out to him. 'I would be glad if you would have this and with it my thanks for your assistance.'

His brows rose and she flushed slightly.

'You may as well take it — it holds but a few guineas. You may be sure I am not giving you my life savings.'

'Then I'll take it, miss, and thank ye kindly.'

He reached out for the purse and at the same time grasped her fingers. Before she realized what he was about he had raised them to his lips, pressing a kiss upon her glove with the practised ease of a courtier. Startled, she snatched her hand away, wondering why his actions had unnerved her more than her encounter with the two ruffians. A shout caused her to look round and she saw her parents hurrying towards her.

'Madeleine, why this delay? What is going on here?' Mr Sedgewick looked at her anxiously.

'My skirt was caught on a splinter and I fell

behind, Papa. Pray do not fear, sir, I am unharmed. Two sailors tried to waylay me and this man saw them off.'

'Then I am in your debt, sir!' exclaimed Mr Sedgewick, turning to the stranger.

'Nay, sir,' he held up the purse. 'The young lady has rewarded me amply.'

He tugged at his forelock, a servile gesture that Madeleine thought quite at variance with the quizzical gleam in his eyes as they rested upon her. She looked away, angry with herself for the blush she could feel spreading over her cheeks.

Mr Sedgewick nodded and took his daughter's arm.

'Well, well then. No more to be said. We will bid you goodday, my man, for there's urgent business we must attend to. Come along, ladies, we must hurry to the quayside if we are not to miss my nephew.'

'Papa!' Miss Sedgewick hurried alongside her father, 'Were you not a little brusque with that man? After all, he rendered me a signal service.'

'Perhaps, child, perhaps, but we are in a hurry and you had already given him your purse. How much was in it, by the by?'

'Oh, I know not — a guinea or two.'

'It seems so little reward for his efforts,' observed Mrs Sedgewick. 'He did not look to be a very prosperous person, yet perhaps it may do him some good.'

'One would hope so, my dear,' said her husband, 'but I think it much more likely that the fellow will squander it at the first ale house he comes to.'

Mr Sedgewick made a grab for his hat as he finished speaking, for they had reached the waterfront where there was no shelter from the blustery wind. He hurried the ladies along the quay towards the bustle of activity taking place beside the packet, which was by this time safely moored.

'I think I see him!' cried Mr Sedgewick.

He guided the ladies towards a lone figure, standing a little apart from the general crowd. The man was wrapped in a dark surtout, its collar turned up and his hat pulled so low that very little of his countenance was exposed to the chill wind.

'Sir, if you will excuse me, M. le Comte?'

The stranger turned and a flash of white was visible between the hat brim and the collar.

'*Ah, mon oncle Sedgewick, n'est-ce pas?*' He removed his hat and made a flourishing bow, 'Camille du Vivière, at your service, *monsieur.*'

Mr Sedgewick grasped his hand and shook it vigorously.

'Camille, my boy, it's very good to see you here at last! You remember your aunt, of course, but perhaps you will not recognize this young lady, eh?'

He drew Madeleine forward and the *comte*'s dark eyes rested upon her for a moment, then with a smile he took her hand and raised it to his lips.

'Madeleine, I could not mistake you.'

'Then your memory is better than mine, *monsieur*, since I cannot in truth say I remember *you* at all!' she replied laughingly.

'Ah, but you were then a babe, were you not, when we last met?'

'I was all of five years, sir, but you were more than twice my age, and very grown up, as you never ceased to inform me.'

He squeezed her fingers, smiling ruefully.

'Was I indeed so insolent? It was bad of me, but now I will allow you to be very grown up, and very beautiful, too.'

Madeleine laughed and blushed. She wanted to tease him by saying that she had grown up to be as tall as he, but their acquaintance was too new to risk such a joke. She was grateful to her father for his suggestion that they remove from the area.

'We have rooms at a local inn for tonight,' he continued, taking the Frenchman by the arm and preparing to lead him away, 'I

11

thought it best that we all get a good night's rest before travelling on to Stapley in the morning. Is that your only trunk? Just a moment and I'll have one of these fellows carry it to the Three Barrels . . . '

While Mr Sedgewick and the *comte* went off to find a porter, his wife took the opportunity of a quiet word with her daughter.

'Well, what a pleasant surprise. Whoever would have thought that your cousin would achieve such pleasing manners — he was such a proud, odious little boy.'

'He certainly seems to have changed for the better.'

'And so very personable,' pursued Mrs Sedgewick. 'I fear he will create something of a stir amongst the young ladies of the neighbourhood.'

'That need not worry us, Mama! Since Grandpapa never allows us to entertain at Stapley Hall, no one will have the chance to meet Camille.'

'I very much fear you are right,' agreed her mama sadly, 'but perhaps it is not such a bad thing after all, for the poor young man cannot be said to be a very eligible *parti*, can he? And until some sort of order can be brought about in France — and it is no good anyone telling me that the Convention has any proper control, not when people are turned out of houses that have been in their family for generations and forced to fly the country, to say nothing of imprisoning their own king! No, as long as those detestable people are in power I fear your poor cousin can have little chance of regaining his estates.' She sighed. 'But there it is, we cannot change the situation. Now, here comes Camille. He can escort you back to the inn and you must do your best to keep him amused, poor young man, he has had such a sad time of it.'

'But I hardly know him, Mama — ' Madeleine's protest was brushed aside.

'You are never at a loss for words when you meet your grandfather, and if you can stand up to him without trembling, I am sure you can entertain a pleasant young man for a few minutes! Hush now. Here he comes.'

There was no time for further protest. Mrs Sedgewick took up her position beside her husband, leaving Madeleine to accept the *comte*'s escort. It did not displease her to have her cousin's company. On the contrary, she found his diffidence very engaging, but having been instructed to amuse him, she could think of nothing entertaining to say and thus it was that after a few moments her companion was moved to enquire if he had in some way offended.

'No, of course not, Monsieur le Comte!'

'Ah — it is perhaps the mode for English ladies to walk along in silence and looking so very serious?'

She smiled at this but shook her head.

'Not at all. In fact, I am failing in my duty, Monsieur le Comte. I should be amusing you with an endless flow of small talk, but alas I can think of nothing to say.'

'A situation that will be remedied, I trust, when we are better acquainted. And perhaps we may begin by dispensing with formality. I will not have you call me 'Monsieur le Comte' a moment longer — it must be Camille, if you please or' — he temporized, sensing her hesitation — 'at the very least 'cousin'.'

She laughed.

'Very well, Cousin! Only tell me what you would like to talk about and I will do my best to accommodate you.'

'Tell me of yourself,' he said promptly.

She looked at him, puzzled.

'My mother and yours were regular correspondents. There can be very little that you do not already know.'

'I regret that I paid very little attention to any news from England in the past,' he confessed. 'My English relatives were never of great interest to me — until now.'

14

'It is very sad that you should be forced to quit your home so suddenly. It must have been a terrible wrench for you.'

'One can only be thankful that *ma mère* did not live to know of our loss — it would have broken her heart, I think.'

'We were all very sorry to hear of her death. It was some comfort to Mama that Charles could convey to you our deepest sympathy.'

'Charles?'

'Charles Lacy — Mama's cousin. He had business in Dijon in November last year and Mama received your letter a week or so before he was due to leave London. Thus she was able to contact him and give him her letters for safe delivery to you.'

He shook his head, putting a hand over his eyes.

'Ah, of course. There were so many callers at that time — '

Forgetting her shyness, Madeleine clutched at his arm.

'Excuse me, Cousin. I did not mean to revive painful memories for you.'

'No, no, I assure you I am not reluctant to talk of these things. Where is Charles now? Shall I have the pleasure of meeting him again?'

'Oh, I very much doubt it. He is in Italy at

present — at least, that is where he was when he last wrote to Mama.' she replied, her eyes twinkling. 'Charles is an inveterate traveller. I believe his intention was to go on to Switzerland, but if he should chance to meet up with anyone travelling to Egypt, or Greece, in all likelihood he would change his plans in an instant!'

'A most unpredictable fellow!' Camille smiled. He looked up. 'The Three Barrels — is this where we are to stay?'

'Yes. The landlord is very agreeable, but do not be alarmed if his wife appears uncivil — our host assured us upon our arrival that she has a heart of gold, but does not like to show it. However, she keeps an *excellent* table.'

'In that case,' declared the *comte*, 'I can forgive her any incivility, for I have a great hunger. Let us go in!'

2

The party set off for Stapley the following day in the ageing travelling carriage that Sir Joseph still considered suitable for family outings. It was slow transport, but commodious, with ample space for four passengers. As the coach stood in the yard of the inn, ready loaded and awaiting the travellers, the landlady regarded it with patent disapproval. She shook her head at Miss Sedgewick, who had just emerged from the inn.

'I don't like it, miss, and so I tell you!'

Madeleine blinked. 'I beg your pardon?'

'I don't like to think of you settin' off from 'ere without a proper guard — not when the country's so full of foreigners.'

'Now, now, Mrs Sacher, what's that?' demanded Mr Sedgewick, coming up to them. 'What is it you are saying about foreigners?'

'I was just telling Miss Sedgewick that it ain't safe to leave 'ere without an armed escort, sir. I've heard the tales, you know.' She nodded sagely. 'There's gangs of these Frenchies wanderin' abroad, pretending to be poor souls fleeing for their lives, but they're just waiting to pounce on unsuspecting travellers. French spies, they are, sent over 'ere to terrorize good English folk.'

'Fiddlesticks!' declared Mr Sedgewick impatiently. 'These poor wretches deserve all our sympathy, my good woman! Such suspicions are dangerous nonsense.'

'You think there is no truth in what she says, Papa?' asked Madeleine, as she climbed into the carriage.

'None at all, my dear. The wretched country has gone mad with its talk of spies and revolutionaries. Rest assured we shall be safe enough. Jack Coachman has Gubbins up beside him with the shotgun. That will suffice. Now, what has happened to your mama? I told her I wanted to be away by eleven and it is already ten minutes past the hour.'

Even as he spoke, Mrs Sedgewick came hurrying out of the inn attended by the Comte du Vivière. A few moments' bustle and they were all settled into their seats and ready to set off.

As the coach lumbered out of the yard, the comte looked faintly surprised.

'Do your attendants follow later with the luggage, sir?'

'Oh, there is no one else to come, my boy,' explained Mr Sedgewick. 'All our baggage is

18

strapped up behind, so we do not require a second carriage.'

'Do you think, Cousin, that we cannot manage for a few days without an array of attendants?' Madeleine quizzed him gently. 'You have a very poor opinion of the English.'

'I beg your pardon — when I heard you say that you have already been a week in Tonbridge — '

'Aunt Halley has servants enough for all of us, so Grandpapa was spared the expense of sending our own people in a second carriage.'

'Madeleine, my dear! You should not speak of your grandfather as though he were ungenerous.' Mrs Sedgewick uttered a mild rebuke.

'Well, we all know that he holds the purse-strings,' came the frank reply.

'Oh, that reminds me.' Mr Sedgewick reached into his pocket. 'I have to return this to you.'

Madeleine reached across to take the purse he held out to her, looking at her father in some bewilderment. He smiled.

'I was about to retire last night when I bumped into your rescuer coming out of the tap-room — no mistaking the fellow with those broad shoulders and that mane of hair! He said he'd been looking for our party, because he wanted to return the young lady's purse, although if you were to ask me, I'd say that was merely an excuse made up on the spur of the moment when he saw I'd recognized him; it's much more likely that he'd been drinking his money away.'

'Whatever the circumstances, I am pleased to have my purse back. Although I must say,' added Madeleine, surveying the article doubtfully, 'it looks a trifle the worse for wear; in fact it is decidedly grubby! I shall give it to Sarah when we get back: she must see what can be done with it.'

'What is this, Cousin?' exclaimed the *comte*, his face alive with concern, 'Did you lose your purse?'

'No, no, much worse than that!' put in Mrs Sedgewick.

'*Mon Dieu!* You will tell me.'

'Oh it was not so very bad.' Madeleine blushed faintly, 'I was accosted by two ruffians while wc were on our way to the quayside yesterday. I had fallen rather behind Mama and Papa and they took advantage of the situation to bar my way. Thankfully a third man came along and saw them off. As a token of my gratitude I gave him my purse: he looked in need of a few extra guineas.'

'And indeed they were well deserved!' cried her cousin, with such a sparkling look that she found herself blushing even more.

'But I had the right of it when I said the fellow would drink away his reward. I spotted him on the quay only minutes after the incident, talking to the sailors from the packet. Doubtless they shared in his good fortune.' Mr Sedgewick pondered the matter for a while, then he settled himself comfortably into his corner, closed his eyes and almost immediately began to snore gently.

Observing this, the *comte* looked across at Miss Sedgewick and lifted a quizzical eyebrow. Madeleine's hazel eyes twinkled responsively.

'Papa finds journeys very tedious.'

'And his good lady follows him, I see, as in all things.'

Madeleine glanced at her mama, dozing quietly in her corner.

'I find it amazing that anyone can sleep in a carriage: one is constantly being jolted and jarred.'

'You dislike travelling, Cousin Madeleine?'

'On the contrary, I enjoy it.'

'Even if you are, as you say, being jolted and jarred!'

She laughed. 'Even that! Admittedly long journeys can be tedious, but Mama cannot travel for more than a few hours at a time and I never tire of watching the changing countryside.'

'Shall we reach Stapley tonight?'

'No. We go only as far as Uckfield today and on to Stapley in the morning. We travel by easy stages, but we should be home in time for dinner tomorrow.'

'I am so looking forward to seeing my grandfather. You look surprised — have I said something wrong, Cousin?'

'Not exactly, but no one looks *forward* to meeting Sir Joseph.'

'Is he so terrible?' he asked her wryly.

'He makes a habit of being disagreeable!' She cast a guilty look towards her parents, who were both sleeping peacefully. 'Perhaps it is wrong of me to speak so of Grandfather, but I would rather you were prepared. He dislikes company, so we have very few visitors, and although I believe Papa has many acquaintances in Town — he works in government, you know — he does not invite them to Stapley for fear that Grandpapa will be rude to them! I cannot believe he means the half of it, but he does say the most cutting things. You cannot have forgotten that your previous visit to us was curtailed after Sir Joseph quarrelled with your papa.'

'Over the years one's memories fade, I believe, but, Cousin — *you* surely do not remember it!'

'No, Mama told me of it, how she and

Papa posted from London only to find that your father had decided to leave that very day. They saw you both for only a few minutes before you left the house.'

'Let us hope this time my stay will be a protracted one.' He smiled. 'I promise you I shall not be easily driven away.'

Once again Madeleine felt the colour rising to her cheeks, while a sensation not altogether unpleasant stirred within her: it could not be denied that she felt herself drawn towards her cousin. His features were finely carved, the skin smooth, though its pallor was emphasized by the raven-black hair which he wore unpowdered and tied back with a single ribbon. However, it was the eyes that had first caught Madeleine's attention. They were dark, almost black, yet vitally expressive, providing a striking contrast in an otherwise calm countenance and the expression in them at that moment was so openly admiring that she was at once flattered and alarmed.

To bring the conversation back to safer ground, she said, 'No indeed! I should think very poorly of you if you allowed Grandpapa to bully you! It merely makes him worse, you know. He likes people to stand up to him.'

'Thank you for your advice, Cousin,' came the grave reply, 'I shall endeavour to adhere to it.'

3

'Grandpapa? Do you want you be alone? I
can go away again if you wish ... ?'
Madeleine hesitated at the drawing-room
door. It was the family's custom to gather
there before dinner and Madeleine had come
down earlier than usual, expecting to find the
room empty. Instead, she found Sir Joseph
sitting in a wing chair beside the fire. He had
been a fine-looking man in his youth, and his
bearing was still upright although he now
needed the aid of a stick to walk. His gaunt
features and shaggy brows gave him a severe
look that made his daughter-in-law quake,
but Miss Sedgewick had never been afraid of
her grandfather, and although she hesitated at
the door there was no hint of timidity in her
voice. Sir Joseph waved at her to come
forward.

'No, no, come along in, child. Pour me a
glass of wine, there's a good girl. We've an
hour at least until dinner. And fill it up, girl, I
want no half measures from you.'

'The doctor said you were to reduce the
amount you drink,' she reminded him, resolutely putting down the decanter and holding

out a half-filled glass, which he waved away.

'Damn the doctor!' he retorted irascibly, 'And damn you if you don't fill it up. For heaven's sake, girl, I'll drink what I like at the dinner-table, so it makes precious little odds.'

'*Then* it will be your own fault if your gout becomes worse,' she told him, quite unmoved by his intemperate language, 'but I'll not flaunt Dr Gower's advice. Besides,' she added saucily, 'when your leg is painful it puts you in the devil's own temper.'

'That's nothing to the rage you will drive me to if you don't do as you are told.'

'You observe me shaking with terror.'

For a moment he glowered at her, but she returned his look steadily and at last he laughed and took the glass from her.

'Od's fish, girl, you're a cool one!'

'Not at all. I've lived all my life with your rantings and I set very little store by them.'

'Are you out with me because I spoke my mind to that French grandson o'mine?' he barked, watching her through narrowed eyes.

'You were downright rude to him!' she retorted. 'Your comments upon his mother were particularly insensitive.'

'I merely told him she had more hair than wit to marry a foreigner — damme I'd have said the same thing to her face!'

'That thought is not likely to comfort

25

Camille — the poor young man has suffered horribly this past year.'

'I can't say I noticed him looking particularly grief-stricken.'

'It does not surprise me, in the face of your hostility.'

Sir Joseph's eyes snapped.

'Damme, girl, this is my house and I shall do as I please in it! The fellow should be grateful to have a roof over his head, and if he don't care for my comments he is at liberty to take his leave whenever he wishes — 'twould be one less mouth to feed!'

Madeleine's heart sank: her grandfather was in one of his difficult moods and seemed to have taken his grandson in dislike. She did her best to coax him into a better humour, but had only partially succeeded when her parents appeared, and with them, the *comte*. There was nothing more to be done. Madeleine went to sit beside her mother while the gentlemen made themselves comfortable on the other side of the fireplace, where the warming blaze crackled cheerfully. Mr Sedgewick engaged the *comte* in conversation and Madeleine had begun to hope that Sir Joseph's ill-humour might have spent itself when a chance remark about France brought the old gentleman out of his reverie.

26

'Aye, the French are a bad lot — never liked 'em above half. And what a state they are in now, eh? That Irishman Burke had the right of it: he said how it would be if the Frenchies were allowed to go on unchecked! There's a pack of upstarts calling themselves a National Assembly and trying to overrun the rest of Europe, while here in England we are overrun with *émigrés*!'

Mr Sedgewick shifted uncomfortably in his seat and gave a nervous laugh.

'Oh come now, sir, I think you are being a little harsh,' he said, trying to make light of the matter. 'I am sure the unfortunate people who have fled their country would be only too thankful to return, if they could.'

'If they had taken better care of their country in the first place they would not have been forced to quit it!' retorted the old man. He fixed his fierce eyes on his grandson, 'What do you say to all this, sir?'

'Oh no, Grandpapa!' cried Miss Sedgewick, jumping up. 'It is unfair to expect the *comte* to give you an opinion, when you are so outspoken.'

'On the contrary, Cousin. In some respects I must agree with Sir Joseph.'

'Oh, you must, eh?' muttered the old gentleman, eyeing him with obvious dislike.

'I cannot argue with you when you say

France was mismanaged in the past. For centuries she has been worn down by weak government and corruption, but I think I can reassure you on one point, sir. Most of the émigrés, including myself, would be only too glad to leave England if it were safe to do so.' He paused. 'Your country is far too cold for us.'

His words hung in the silence as everyone waited for Sir Joseph's reaction. The old man stared hard at his grandson, then he nodded, a little less disapproving than before, thought Madeleine.

'Then the sooner we go to war and settle the issue, the better for all of us. Fill my glass again, George. Damme, where is Kershaw? Dinner should be ready by now.'

Mr Sedgewick carried Sir Joseph's glass to the side table where the half-filled decanter rested on its silver tray. He made a wry face at his daughter as he passed her chair.

'The young fellow carried that off neatly,' he said softly. 'At least he gave your grandfather no reason to order him out of the house.'

'But why does he have to provoke everyone who comes here?' she muttered angrily.

'He likes to show us that he is master,' responded her father. 'Young Camille handled himself pretty well, I thought. Very cool, wasn't he? Surprised me, I'll admit. I thought he'd fire up and say something rash — his father was somewhat hot-tempered, I recall, and his mama would never think before speaking! But the boy had himself well under control. Still, it will be dashed awkward for the poor fellow if his face don't fit. Which reminds me, I'd better give him the hint that m'father can't abide table talk: that *would* put the old fellow out of sorts and we should all be in the suds!'

The *comte* having been thus warned to avoid unnecessary chatter, nothing untoward occurred to upset Sir Joseph's dinner and if the silence was a little daunting, Madeleine did her best to encourage her cousin with an occasional friendly smile across the table. She received her reward when the gentlemen came into the drawing-room later, for the *comte* made his way directly to her side.

'You are early,' she greeted him, 'I had not expected to see any of you for another hour yet.'

He grimaced.

'*Mademoiselle*, you alarm me. In the event I was beginning to doubt that I could endure much longer without your smiles to support me.'

'Oh come, sir, I am sure you are very well able to take care of yourself.'

'Camille, will you take tea?' Mrs Sedgewick's

enquiry denied him the chance to reply and he moved away to return moments later carrying two cups.

'And when will you be returning to London, Cousin?' he asked, handing Madeleine her tea.

'Oh we spend very little time in Town.'

'But this I do not understand. Is not my uncle obliged to be in London a great deal? He is in government, is he not?'

'Well, yes. He holds a minor post at the Foreign Office, but he has only rooms for himself in Town. Mama and I stay here, and Papa travels to Stapley as often as he can manage. Grandpapa will not hear of our setting up home anywhere else, and Papa will not go against his wishes.' She stopped guiltily. 'Do I sound very bitter? I should not complain. I had one London Season before Grandpapa shut up the Town house last winter, after Uncle Robert's accident.'

'Oh? Your uncle was injured?'

Madeleine put down her cup and stared at him. She said quietly, 'He broke his neck. I know Mama wrote to you . . . '

He looked stunned, then rubbed one white hand across his eyes.

'Cousin, I beg you will forgive me. Last winter was one of such sadness, my mother's long illness, and her blessed release in

December — I fear my senses were very much disordered then.'

Impulsively she put out her hand to him.

'Of course, Camille. I understand. Please believe you have all my sympathy. Such troubles you have had this past twelve months. I only wish I could do something to help.'

He squeezed her hand and smiled at her earnest face.

'Your compassion already helps me, as does your beauty, Cousin.'

She gently freed her hand from his grasp and rose, her eyes twinkling.

'The years have certainly silvered your tongue, Cousin,' she said. 'My glass tells me I am passable, no more.' She put up her hand as he was about to speak, 'No, pray do not contradict me, for *that* would cast doubt upon my reason.'

Before he could reply, Mr Sedgewick walked up to them, demanding to know if they were quarrelling.

'Not at all, sir,' responded the *comte*, smiling. 'Your daughter has brought me to an impasse. I may not compliment her upon her appearance, which she says is merely passable, yet to agree with her on that point would be an insult.'

'Undoubtedly it would!' returned Mr

31

Sedgewick jovially, 'But you do not do yourself justice, Maddie! Why, you have grown into a fine, healthy young woman. Good eyes and teeth, a fine head of hair — '

'You talk as though I were a horse!' she objected, laughing. 'I see that I shall find no sense in either of you tonight, so I shall go away.'

'Yes, go away and help your mama — she is playing backgammon with your grandfather and faring terribly, of course.'

'That is because she allows him to bully her,' replied Madeleine. 'I shall go to her aid and let us hope that between us we can keep Grandpapa happy until bedtime.'

★ ★ ★

The party broke up early that evening: Sir Joseph was not in the habit of keeping late hours and the others, after a day and a half spent travelling, were only too glad to follow his example. Yet it was a long time before Madeleine slept. She dismissed her maid and sat for a long while before her mirror. Her hair, released from its pins, curled around her face and down on to her shoulders. From the glass, a pale, rather serious face gazed back at her framed by an abundance of honey-brown hair that fell softly to her shoulders. Dark brows arched above hazel eyes that looked out fearlessly upon the world. A straight nose led down to a mouth that was too generous for beauty. Yes, 'merely passable' was a very apt description! With something very like a sigh she extinguished the candles on her dressing-table and, slipping out of her wrap, she climbed quickly into bed and snuffed out her bedside candle. In the darkness she lay thinking about her French cousin: he was certainly very charming and it was gratifying that he should be so attentive, but Madeleine's instinct urged caution. Here was a young man who had lost everything he held most dear and incredibly he seemed to have sur-mounted his misfortunes very well, but was it not possible that his attraction to herself was nothing more than a reaction against these troubles? Indeed it seemed the only solution, for it would argue a want of sensibility if the *comte* were merely trying to get up a flirtation with her. Madeleine was troubled. She had always considered herself a good judge of people, but her cousin Camille baffled her.

'What do you expect?' she asked herself drowsily, 'you have known him barely two days — to learn everything about a person in so short a time would be impossible, unless he was incredibly dull!' Camille's handsome face floated in her memory: she recalled the tremor of excitement she had felt when she had surprised an admiring gleam in his eyes. No, she hugged herself, smiling. There was nothing dull about her French cousin.

4

If Miss Sedgewick had hoped the following day would give her leisure to become better acquainted with her cousin, she was to be disappointed. She emerged from her bed-chamber to find Mrs Sedgewick hurrying past her door with her arms full of bedding.

'Mama, what is all this?' she asked, falling into step beside her distracted parent.

'Oh Madeleine my dear, you are just the person I need! Take these along to the Red Room, my love. You will find Bessie there making up the bed. I must go and see cook — Kershaw tells me he has flown into one of his rages and is threatening to leave this instant. Of course he would never do so, for your grandfather pays him very handsomely, but nevertheless I must do what I can to restore order in the kitchen.'

'Oh Mama! Pray do not rush off without telling me what is afoot.'

'Oh 'tis the most ridiculous thing. When Bessie came in with my hot chocolate this morning she brought a message from your grandfather saying that Sir Thomas Wyre is calling today.'

'My godfather, calling here? How splendid! But why such short notice?'

'It appears that Sir Joseph had word from him yesterday morning, but forgot to mention it. It is all very well for you to laugh, Maddie, but there is not a thing prepared.'

'I am sorry, Mama, but surely the house-keeper can deal with all these arrangements.'

Mrs Sedgewick gave her daughter a pained look.

'Mrs Porten is visiting her sister in Leatherhead,' she explained patiently. 'You may remember I told you yesterday that I had given her leave to go — of course, that was before I knew of Sir Thomas's visit.'

'How long does he stay? Will Lady Wyre and Cassie be with him?'

'No, Sir Thomas is coming alone, and will be here for dinner, but, of course, I shall ask him to stay over — I would not expect him to travel on to Wyre Hall tonight. It is all of five and twenty miles and in the dark, too!'

Madeleine laughed.

'Do you mean all this bustle is for an extra bed for one night? Why, Sir Thomas is such an old friend of the family, I am sure he would not want you to trouble yourself so.'

'That may well be so, but I would not have him find us wanting in hospitality,' replied Mrs Sedgewick, bristling with housewifely pride, 'It must not be said that Stapley cannot function properly merely because the house-keeper is away. Now, will you please take these sheets along to Bessie and after that — '

'After that, I shall break my fast,' Miss Sedgewick interrupted her. 'If you need my services later, dear Mama, I am at your disposal, but first I must eat.'

True to her word, as soon as she had breakfasted, Madeleine went in search of her mother and began to tackle some of the numerous tasks that Mrs Sedgewick considered it necessary to complete, if their visitor was to be comfortable at Stapley. She learned from Sarah, her maid, of Sir Thomas's arrival, but it was not until dinner-time that she had the pleasure of meeting him. Madeleine chose for the occasion a dress of cream flowered silk worn over a glazed wool petticoat, around her shoulders she arranged a soft rose-coloured cashmere shawl, which fulfilled the dual purpose of adding a touch of colour to her appearance and keeping her warm, for Sir Joseph did not care to waste his money keeping too many fires burning at Stapley.

⋆   ⋆   ⋆

She found Sir Thomas and her parents in the drawing-room, seated close to the blazing fire

37

that crackled merrily in the hearth. With his brown bag-wig and full skirted coat of burgundy velvet, Sir Thomas looked every bit the prosperous country gentleman, which indeed he was. His more ambitious wife would have liked to spend more time in Town, but Sir Thomas openly acknowledged that he disliked socializing. Despite his connection with some of the highest families in the land, he preferred to live quietly at Wyre Hall with his wife and daughter, entertaining his closest friends and improving his estates. The gentlemen rose as she entered, Sir Thomas holding out his hands, saying: 'Madeleine, my dear child. Have you a kiss for your godfather?'

'A dozen!' she replied, taking his hands and planting a kiss upon his rough cheek. 'How do you do, sir?'

'Oh I am very well, my dear. But let me look at you. By Jove, Maddie, you are looking very well. I do believe you have grown a little since I last saw you.'

'Oh do not say so!' she cried, throwing up her hands in mock dismay. 'Why, I am as tall as Papa now; any more and I shall be labelled a freak.'

'Oh Madeleine, pray do not exaggerate,' interrupted her mama, laughing. 'Come and sit down, child, and try if you can to persuade our guest to prolong his visit.'

'No, I am sorry, it is impossible.' He shook his head as Miss Sedgewick's eyes turned earnestly towards him. 'There were a few business papers for your father to see and when Grenville heard I was coming this way, he asked if I would drop them by.'

'Is there any news, sir?' said Madeleine, 'Does Papa have to go back to Town?'

'No, no, nothing like that, my dear. These papers are merely to keep me up to date.'

'Those poor French people coming to our shores seeking refuge are bringing the most chilling tales,' put in Mrs Sedgewick. 'I heard any number of horrifying stories while we were at Rye and now everyone seems to fear that there are French spies running all over the countryside.'

'I don't know about that,' replied Sir Thomas, 'but reports are coming in from Holland that the French are stirring up trouble in the villages there.'

'We have an alliance with the Dutch, do we not? We are honour bound to help them, if they are attacked.'

Sir Thomas cast an admiring glance at his goddaughter.

'Aye, that is so. You are well informed, lass. I hope your father is not passing on any state secrets.'

They all laughed at that and into this cordial atmosphere came Sir Joseph, closely followed by the Comte du Vivière. When Sir Thomas had exchanged civilities with his host, and Camille had been presented to him, there was a momentary lull in the conversation. The time did not seem propitious to resume talk of war with France and instead Mrs Sedgewick asked Sir Thomas for news of his family.

'Does Lady Wyre plan to come to Wyre Hall for the winter?'

'My dear wife remains in London for a while longer, which, by the by, is my reason for dashing away from you so soon. I have a few matters requiring my attention at the Hall, then it is back to town again to escort my family and a party of friends to Wyre for Christmas.'

'You seem less than enchanted with the prospect, sir,' observed Madeleine, her eyes twinkling.

Her godfather shook his head.

'It's not my line at all,' he said glumly. 'My lady wife is sure that she can bring one of Cassandra's suitors up to scratch and to that end she's had me invite a whole crowd of people to the Hall. Says it wouldn't do just to invite young Kilmer — though in my opinion if the fellow's keen enough on m'daughter, he'll propose to her in any case.'

'Oh no, Sir Thomas, Lady Wyre is quite right,' declared Mrs Sedgewick. 'To invite only the young gentleman to stay and for the sole purpose of having him offer for Cassandra would be most detrimental to that young man's affections.'

'Lady Wyre said the same thing,' was the gloomy reply. 'And I suppose you are both right. It does seem a great deal of trouble, though, over one fellow! After all, Cassie's not yet nineteen and if I do say it myself, she's a fine-looking girl so there's no need for her to jump at the first offer to come her way.'

'Who is the gentleman?' asked Mr Sedgewick.

'Lord Kilmer. You probably know him, George.'

'Only vaguely. Member of Brooks's, is he not? Not my crowd, I'm afraid.'

'Nor mine, but at least he's not one of Fox's followers. I'd not countenance a match with such a one, be he never so rich!'

Madeleine smiled.

'And *is* Lord Kilmer very wealthy, if one may enquire about such a vulgar matter?'

'As a nabob! The catch of the season, I'm told, if she can pull it off.'

'Poor Sir Thomas!'

'Oh it ain't that I dislike the fellow — quite

41

the reverse, in fact, but to be obliged to invite a host of people to stay, when I'm not above nodding terms with the half of 'em, seems to me a great piece of work!'

'A great piece of nonsense is what it is!' put in Sir Joseph acidly. 'You allow your womenfolk to rule the roost, Wyre. You should take a firm stand now, sir, or they'll ruin you, damme if they don't!'

Well used to Sir Joseph's sharp manner, Sir Thomas merely smiled, saying mildly, 'I know, sir, I know — I am too easy-going. I am often told it is so, but what am I to do? If it keeps my dear lady happy to have a houseful of guests then so be it, I'll not deny her that pleasure.'

'For my part I'd as lief be left alone,' muttered Sir Joseph, with a sidelong glance at the *comte*. 'The more people there are in a house, the more disturbance they make, to say nothing of the expense!'

Miss Sedgewick could only be glad that Camille was at that moment engaged in conversation with her father and had moved away, so that he did not hear Sir Joseph's utterance. With his usual good humour her godfather turned off the remark with a light-hearted comment and went on to talk of other matters. After dinner Sir Thomas joined his host and Mr and Mrs Sedgewick for a rubber of whist, leaving Madeleine to entertain her cousin.

The young people were soon deep in conversation and they continued thus until the card party broke up and the two ladies retired from the drawing-room together.

'Well, the evening passed off much better than I dared hope,' remarked Mrs Sedgewick as she started up the stairs beside her daughter. 'I am sorry that you and Camille could not enjoy a little more of Sir Thomas's company after dinner, but your grandfather insisted we play at cards.'

'One could hardly expect him to pass up the opportunity of having a skilled partner, Mama. You know how critical he is if you or I partner him.'

'Which is most unfair of him. I confess I am not at my best when playing cards with Sir Joseph, but to be treated like an imbecile is almost beyond bearing. However,' she continued, recollecting her original theme, 'I do not think Camille felt any lack of company tonight. Every time I looked over, the two of you were engrossed in conversation.'

'It was a most enjoyable evening, Mama, but for all our talking, I still know very little of our cousin. In fact, I think I did most of the talking! He was very keen to learn about the family.'

'Poor boy, doubtless he shies away from his painful memories at present. I am sure I cannot blame him. He will be more forthcoming in time.'

'If Grandpapa does not drive him away!'

They had arrived at Madeleine's door and stopped.

'That same thought had occurred to me,' sighed Mrs Sedgewick. 'One can only hope your grandfather will come round a little when he knows Camille better.'

'But why has he taken Camille in such dislike? It is inexplicable.'

'Perhaps it is because your cousin is now heir to Stapley.'

She saw her daughter's look of surprise and continued, 'The inheritance passes to the nearest male relative. When your Uncle Robert was alive, it was assumed he would eventually marry and have a quiverful of children to continue the line. Now, of course, your father will take over when Sir Joseph is gone, but as we have no son the *comte* would be the next in line.'

Madeleine's eyes twinkled with merriment.

'And he does so dislike 'Frenchies' as he calls them. Poor Grandpapa.'

'Yes, and poor Camille, too. I only hope Sir Joseph does not make his position here untenable.'

Miss Sedgewick rose early the following morning to say goodbye to Sir Thomas. Her father escorted him to the waiting carriage, but Madeleine paid little attention to their prolonged conversation at the carriage door, merely agreeing with her mama that it did the gentlemen no good at all to be standing about in the damp morning air. At last, Sir Thomas climbed into his seat, the steps were put up and he was away, giving them a final wave of his hand as the coach moved off. Mr Sedgewick returned to the house, beaming broadly.

'Well, sir, I declare you look like a cat that's had the cream!' exclaimed his lady, 'Whatever has Sir Thomas said to put you into such a good humour?'

'Well, now it is all arranged, perhaps it would be as well to tell you.' He chuckled as he ushered the ladies into the morning-room. Two pairs of enquiring eyes were immediately fixed upon him. 'No doubt you would like me to explain,' he began, savouring the attention.

'Indeed we would!'

'We are invited to spend Christmas at Wyre Hall, my dears.'

The effect of this statement was everything he could have wished. His wife sat down upon the nearest chair, staring at him with her mouth opened into a little 'o' of surprise. Madeleine, after a brief moment of disbelief, ran towards him, firing questions.

'But how is this? Was it all arranged this morning, Papa? Are we all to go?'

'Just a moment, my dear!' he laughed, putting up his hands, 'Sit down now and I will tell you the whole. Sir Thomas broached the subject last night, just after you had retired. He is well aware of Sir Joseph's rather — ah — solitary disposition, and when m'father made some remark about having to put up with a houseful of people, Sir Thomas suggested, quite casually, that he'd be glad to relieve him of the burden for a few weeks.'

'And, of course, Grandfather readily agreed! Just think of the savings to his household.'

'Madeleine, you are being uncharitable.' Mrs Sedgewick frowned at her daughter. 'Sir Joseph has never withheld a penny that was necessary to our comfort. To be sure, he does not like *extravagance* — '

'I suppose it would be extravagant to have a fire in here in the mornings,' muttered Madeleine, pulling her shawl a little closer about her. 'I am sorry, Papa. Pray continue.'

'Your Grandfather did *not* readily agree,

Madeleine. In fact, it was Sir Thomas who, having initially spoken in jest, said he would be very pleased to have us join his party at Wyre, since a few familiar faces would help him bear with the crowd of strangers that had been thrust upon him.'

'But what of Camille — what had he to say to all this?' asked Miss Sedgewick.

'He was not present at this time, but Sir Thomas made a point of stressing that the invitation included the *comte*. I think that perhaps he was aware of a slight — tension — between Sir Joseph and his grandson.'

Mrs Sedgewick and her daughter exchanged glances, smiling at this understatement.

'After a little thought, m'father said he would leave the decision to me, that I was quite at liberty to accept the invitation, but that he would be spending Christmas quietly here at Stapley, as was his custom. When the *comte* came in shortly after, I put the suggestion to him and since he had no objection to going with us, I accepted on behalf of us all.'

'And I am so glad you did, dear Papa!' cried Madeleine, jumping up to hug him. 'I was becoming very anxious because Grandpapa did not take to Camille, but now I can be easy, at least for a few weeks.'

Madeleine left the morning-room in high

spirits, just as the *comte* appeared on the stairs.

'Oh Cousin, is it not wonderful news? We are off to Wyre Hall! Papa says we are to go at the end of the month!'

'This pleases you, Cousin Madeleine?' he enquired, as she walked with him to the breakfast-room.

'Most assuredly! Life here at Stapley is for the most part sadly flat and' — she glanced around to assure herself that they were alone — 'enlivened only by Grandpapa's frequent ill-humours! Papa almost never entertains here. The last time he brought visitors to Stapley — a Prussian diplomat and his lady — Grandpapa was so outspoken that it ended in a most embarrassing argument, with the poor man concluding that he was unable to call Grandpapa out because of his 'immense age', which Grandpapa did not like at all!'

The *comte* laughed.

'This is an English custom I do not understand,' he said, taking a seat across the breakfast table from his cousin, 'to bury oneself in the country for such long periods — I could not endure it, I think.'

'Now I know you are joking me, Cousin, for I distinctly recall from my aunt's letters to us that you spent most of your time upon your estates.'

48

'Ah, that was when I was younger and,' he hesitated, before continuing with a wry smile, 'I am ashamed to admit it, but *ma mère* was not informed of every visit I made to Paris. There! I have shocked you, Cousin!'

'Not at all. I can see a kind of wisdom in not informing a parent of an escapade that could only alarm, but it is not my place either to censure or condone such a thing.'

'Then I shall ask you to do neither. Tell me instead what you do here to while away the long winter evenings.'

'We go on very well, Cousin.' she assured him, her eyes dancing. 'Reverend Briggishall is a regular visitor and entertains us with his discourse on the *Frailty of Human Nature*, or some other such thing, and Grandpapa says he plays a very fine game of chess, which is why he is allowed to visit us so regularly. I have no doubt he will be summoned to bear Grandpapa company a great deal more while we are away! Then there is my Aunt Halley and her family. They sometimes spend a few days here on their way to or from London and, of course, Cousin Charles frequently calls here when he is in England. Now you are horror-struck at the thought of living in such a dull place!'

'Not at all,' he said politely. 'And we will be at Wyre Hall in little more than week, will we not? Please. Tell me what I am to expect there. Is Sir Thomas a government man, like my uncle?'

'No, although he often says that he could have a post if he had a mind to it, for he knows everyone of importance in political circles. He is an old friend of Lord Grenville, the Foreign Secretary, you see.'

'And Wyre Hall, it is a large establishment?'

Madeleine settled back in her chair and pondered the question, her head tilted to one side.

'It is everything that Stapley is not. Wyre is a large house — a Palladian villa — with none of the panelling and wainscoting that makes Stapley's apartments so dark. The outstanding impression at Wyre is one of lightness and elegance. And it is surrounded by the most beautiful park. One can enjoy a good day's riding without ever leaving Sir Thomas's land.'

'You know the family well, Cousin?'

She nodded. 'Sir Thomas and Lady Wyre are my godparents. As a child I was frequently their guest and was generally treated as one of the family. Of course all the children are married now, except the youngest.'

'Ah, that one is Cassie, who is to marry the young lord,' he put in, looking pleased with himself.

'Yes. Cassandra. She was always a very pretty, lively girl and I have no doubt her parents expect her to make a brilliant alliance.'

'Is that not what every parent would wish?'

'Well, a good match, certainly.' She sat forward suddenly. 'And if you are thinking that Sir Thomas has had more success in finding suitors for his daughters than Papa did for me, I shall take leave to tell you, sir, that I have received at least two very advantageous offers for my hand.'

'I beg your pardon — pray, Cousin, I meant no insult.'

'No, I am sure you did not,' she replied, laughing, but not unkindly, at his evident confusion. 'But you looked so grave and thoughtful that I could not help but tease you. Was it very bad of me? I am sorry. It was certainly most unbecoming of me to boast of such a thing!'

He smiled faintly.

'Are you never serious, Cousin?'

'Of course! But the prospect of spending Christmas with a large party is a very exciting one, do you not agree?'

'That depends upon one's company.'

'Oh, from what I know of Cassie and Lady Wyre, it is sure to be a fascinating mixture.' She broke off, a sudden frown clouding her

51

eyes. 'But perhaps you would rather not be thrust into company so soon after your arrival. If so only tell me, it is not too late for Papa to cry off — '

'Your concern touches me, Madeleine, but you need not be anxious. I am very happy to go into society, that is if society will accept me.'

'Because you are French? Never forget that your mama was an Englishwoman. And with Sir Thomas and Papa behind you, there are very few who would dare to offer you a rebuff.'

'That is very true,' he murmured. 'I do believe my uncle is going to be very useful to me.'

5

Mr Sedgewick's party arrived at Wyre Hall on the very first day of December. Miss Cassandra Wyre was waiting at the entrance of the Hall to greet them and after the necessary introductions she bore Madeleine away to show her to her room.

'I have asked Mama to put you upstairs in the chamber next to my own. We have not met for such a time, Maddie, and there is so much to tell you! I hope you do not object? Mama thought you might prefer to have a room in the west wing, nearer to your parents . . . '

'No, I have no objections. It will be quite like old times.'

'That is *exactly* what I said to Mama! And, of course, with so many guests here, we would have been hard-pressed to find another bedchamber, unless you were to share a room with Miss Marton, or the Eldwick girls, but I made sure you would not like that! Not,' she added, conscience-stricken, 'that I have anything *against* them, but it is so much more grown up to have a room of one's own, is it not?'

Gravely, Madeleine agreed and listened with such good humour to her young friend's chatter that by the time they reached the seclusion of the room prepared for her guest, Miss Wyre was able to declare that she preferred her dear Madeleine to any of her sisters.

'They are all so — so superior! They treat me as a child, even Jane, who is but two years older than me!'

Madeleine smiled. 'I remember when Jane and I were at school together; she was wont to consider herself a little *superior* to the rest of us.'

'Since she married Westlake she has become unbearable!' exclaimed Cassandra. 'She has been here for little more than a day and already I could scream. But you will judge for yourself later. Thankfully the others cannot come — Elinor and Lucinda are engaged to stay with their husbands' families so that we shall not be bothered by them.' Throwing open the door to a bedchamber, Cassandra dismissed her sisters with an insouciance that made her friend smile. 'This is your room — do you remember?'

'Very well. Already it feels like home!' She took off her bonnet and laid it on the bed, enquiring if all the other guests had yet arrived.

'Yes. Most of them travelled down from London with us three days ago, except Jane and Westlake, who came direct from Devonshire, and of course Beau Hauxwell, who arrived yesterday.' Miss Wyre paused, throwing a considering glance at her friend. Madeleine frowned at her.

'Cassie, what mischief are you brewing now?'

'None, I assure you! Only . . . '

'Yes?'

'Well, the gentleman was most attentive to me in Town, you see, when we were introduced, which was all very flattering, but Mama says that Lord Kilmer is about to propose to me, if all goes well . . . '

'So, you want me to keep Mr — what did you say his name is?'

'Hauxwell.' Cassandra giggled. 'Everyone in Town knows him as Beau Hauxwell — he is *extremely* fashionable!'

'He sounds like a veritable coxcomb! But you wish me to entertain him, leaving the field free for Lord Kilmer to propose to you.'

'Exactly. Oh I *knew* you would understand, Madeleine. He is extremely wealthy, I believe, and considered something of a wit, which should suit you, for you are always funning. Besides,' she laughed, sitting down on the edge of the bed, 'he is also extremely tall.'

'That is certainly a consideration,' laughed Madeleine, retrieving her hat that had narrowly escaped being squashed and putting it safely upon the dressing-table. 'I have no objection to beanpoles. Does he squint?'

'Certainly not.'

'Good, for I do not think I could be happy with a husband who squints.'

Miss Wyre clapped her hands in delight.

'Oh I am so glad you have come, Maddie, for I know how you like a joke.'

'Possibly, but apart from informing me that you have chosen for me a tall husband who does not squint, I am not at all sure what joke I am supposed to be enjoying.'

'Well, Beau Hauxwell is some sort of acquaintance of Papa's, although I cannot recall having met him before last week, when we were introduced at Lady Altringham's rout. That night he spent the whole evening following me around and paying me the most *fulsome* compliments! I was quite flattered, of course, for he is considered a very eligible *parti*, but I much prefer Kilmer. In the end Papa took pity on him and invited him to come here — at such short notice too. Mama thinks it was because Papa was quite out of humour at having so many people coming to Wyre, and none of them his particular friends. However, I think perhaps Papa would like me to marry Mr Hauxwell, although he *knows* I am resolved to have Lord Kilmer. But I have now decided that Beau will do for you.'

'Cassandra, you overwhelm me with your generosity. But I doubt if the gentleman will find anything in *me* to admire, when from what you tell me he is already captivated by *you*. How could a brown spindleshanks such as I am compare favourably with your dark beauty?'

Cassandra giggled. 'Do you really think I am beautiful, Maddie?'

Looking at the dark, sparkling eyes and heart-shaped face with its creamy complexion, Madeleine nodded.

'Undoubtedly. And brunettes are very fashionable this year, I understand.'

'Yes, there is that, of course, but when he discovers I am to marry Kilmer, he will naturally look elsewhere for consolation.'

'Naturally.'

'You do not seem very enthusiastic, Maddie. You should be grateful that I am trying to find you a husband.'

'Even if he is a mooncalf.'

'He is nothing of the sort!' came the indignant retort. 'He is extremely good ton — to be sure his manner is sometimes a little odd, but I understand that he is very popular with the London hostesses. And he's as rich as Croesus.'

'I'm surprised you do not wish to keep this paragon for yourself.'

Miss Wyre showed her friend a shocked countenance.

'Madeleine! I have already *told* you of my attachment to Lord Kilmer. Besides' — she wrinkled her nose — 'I do not understand the half of what he says to me. Which is another reason you would suit, for you were always very bookish!'

Madeleine's eyes twinkled but she shook her head.

'Thank you for the compliment, Cassie, if that is what it was, but I am not on the catch for a husband, especially such an odd fellow as you describe.'

Miss Wyre glanced at her slyly.

'Perhaps you would prefer your cousin the *comte*?'

Observing the tell-tale flush that spread over Miss Sedgewick's cheeks, Cassandra jumped up, clapping her hands.

'I guessed it the moment I set eyes on him. Oh Maddie, he is very handsome, is he not? I vow if it was not for Kilmer I should be half in love with him already. And such a sad history Papa told us — is it true that all his estates in France have been snatched from him by that wicked Convention that claims to rule the country? From the tales one hears your cousin appears fortunate to have escaped with his life.'

'I believe in France all those of noble birth are suspect. However, my cousin is free from such worries now. I believe he hopes to build a new life here in England.'

'And are you going to marry him?'

'Really, Cassie, you go on much too fast,' objected Madeleine, torn between confusion and laughter. 'Camille has been with us for but a few weeks.'

'I have known people fall in love in a se'ennight.'

'So too have I, but that is not the case with me, I assure you.'

Cassandra sighed. 'How disappointing. I thought I had uncovered a romance. However, it cannot be helped and Papa says you are to stay at least until the New Year, so there is no telling what might happen by then. By the by, what will you be wearing tonight? *I* have the most ravishing new dress to wear this evening. It is silk — the most beautiful shade of green over a cream petticoat, and Mama has given me her pearls, so it will look most grown-up, do you not think?'

Madeleine agreed, relieved to turn her

friend's thoughts to a much safer topic. Nevertheless, she had to admit to a curiosity to see the young man Miss Wyre had set her heart on, and also to meet the fashionable Beau Hauxwell.

★ ★ ★

Miss Sedgewick made her way down to the drawing-room before dinner accompanied by Cassandra. She was a little daunted to discover that of the entire party she knew only her host's family, but she was determined to be pleased and to find all her fellow guests most amiable. However, she could not but notice that Mrs Eldwick and her daughters were critically assessing her appearance. This did not disturb her, for she knew that the high-waisted gown of ivory sarcenet was eminently suitable for country wear and although it was not the very highest kick of fashion, she was well aware that that pale colour suited her. When she was presented to Lord Kilmer she regarded him with interest: he was a stout young man of no more than average height, classically fair and with a serious demeanour that was thrown into strong relief against Miss Wyre's bubbling liveliness. Madeleine suspected the sharp contrast contributed no small part to her finding the young man rather dull and she was therefore very guarded when Cassandra took her aside presently and asked what she thought of his lordship.

'You do not like him.' Cassandra pouted and shook out the skirts of her new gown.

'Cassie, I did not say that. We have exchanged barely half-a-dozen words and I will not make a judgement upon such little acquaintance.'

'Oh — very well, but I am sure you will like him when you know him better. Kilmer is not at his best at social gatherings,' Miss Wyre continued, anxious to explain. 'He prefers small family parties, but he is very clever, and kind, and — and sincere!'

'These are very desirable qualities in a husband,' remarked Madeleine gravely.

Miss Wyre giggled, unable to remain serious for long.

'I make him sound very *worthy*, do I not? For my part I am glad he is not an accomplished flirt, like Mr Fulbeck whom you met earlier, or a fashionable wit, like Mr Hauxwell — by the by where is Beau? Everyone else is here now.'

'If he is as foppish as you told me, Cassandra, no doubt he needs to spend an age at his dressing-table and wants to impress us all with his grand entrance.'

'You may well be right, Maddie and we will all know soon enough, for here he comes now.'

Miss Sedgewick turned towards the door, to observe the tall gentleman who paused in the entrance to survey the assembled guests. He certainly presented a very striking figure. His tall form was displayed to advantage in a blue evening coat that fitted perfectly across his broad shoulders and he wore the white waistcoat, black knee-breeches and striped stockings with an air of profound elegance. His light brown hair was unpowdered and cut short so that it barely touched the back of his collar. From all she had heard Madeleine had expected a much more flamboyant character and she was surprised to note that he did not sport an abundance of fobs and seals, the mark of the dandy, but merely wore a heavy gold signet ring on one finger and, from a black ribbon around his neck, a quizzing glass swung gently. He bowed towards his host.

'Dashed sorry to keep you waiting, Sir Thomas,' he drawled, putting up one hand to the snowy folds of his cravat, 'My man had not starched the half of my neckcloths. Can you imagine! It has taken me an age to find one that would look even tolerable in company.'

A murmur of laughter rippled across the

room. Madeleine turned away, saying just one word as she passed Miss Wyre, 'Fop!'

She moved towards her father, who was standing beside the Comte du Vivière.

'Well, Maddie, have you been talking non-stop with young Cassandra since you arrived here?'

'Yes, Papa, and even now we have not caught up with all the news!' She turned to her cousin, 'How is your room, Camille? You are in the west wing, I think. I hope you are comfortable.'

'Thank you, Cousin, it is — how do you say it? — full of luxury.'

'Luxury, my dear M. le Comte?' cried Sir Thomas, coming up at that moment, 'No, no, sir, you are being too kind. The apartment is but bachelor fare, and surely not a whit as sumptuous as your *château*, eh, *m'sieur*? Ah — pardon me — that was ill said, when you are unlikely to see your home again for some time. Forgive me!'

'Willingly, Sir Thomas, since I know your words were kindly meant.'

'Just so, my dear sir, just so! Now, what did I come over for? Ah yes, of course, I wanted to make sure you had met everyone before we went in to dinner and here is Mr Hauxwell approaching, eager to be acquainted with you.' He drew that gentleman forward and made the introductions in his bluff, good-natured way. Madeleine found herself looking up into a pair of lazy blue eyes that seemed to be mocking her, but before she could speak, Sir Thomas continued, 'Mr Hauxwell has recently returned from Europe and he tells me he spent some time in France. You will have much to talk of, M. le Comte.'

The Frenchman inclined his head, then glanced an enquiry at Mr Hauxwell.

'You know France well, *m'sieur*?'

'Indeed, sir, 'tis like a second home to me. I am quite desolated by the present troubles.' He paused before adding softly, 'The very best tailors are in Paris, you see. *Now* I shall be obliged to buy my next coat from London.'

Observing the angry flush upon her cousin's cheek, Madeleine broke in hastily. She said archly, 'But tell me, Mr Hauxwell — for a gentleman of fashion, would you not prefer to be in Town for the winter? When one is so conscious of appearance, surely the country must be something of a trial. There is so much mud.'

'Madeleine!' Mr Sedgewick frowned at his daughter, appalled by her ill-manners, but the gentleman merely smiled, his blue eyes glinting as they rested upon her face.

'Ah, yes. The mud. It is certainly a

consideration, but, after all, when one is so admirably entertained indoors, there is no necessity to step outside.'

Sir Thomas laughed heartily.

'Egad, sir, of course you need not go out, but if that spirited creature you keep in my stables ain't up to his withers in mud tomorrow, then I'm a Dutchman! Never seen such a powerful brute. What is it, a Prussian breed?'

'No, Limousin.'

'Ah. A heavy hunter,' put in Mr Sedgewick. 'Half-Arab, I suppose. I hear they are breeding some pretty fine horses in that area of France now.'

Sir Thomas nodded knowledgeably, 'Wait till you see him, George. Beautiful creature, broad chest, beautiful action — haven't seen him jump yet, of course . . . '

Seeing her father and godfather thus engaged in talking horseflesh with Mr Hauxwell, Madeleine took her cousin's arm and led him gently away.

'I think we can safely leave them to their horses, Camille. Pray do not allow that foolish man to anger you.'

'He did not — or at least, only for a moment. But I do not know why he should wish to provoke me.'

She frowned. 'Nor I, Cousin and I vow it

makes me ashamed of my countrymen.'

The *comte* smiled at her vehemence.

'Hush, Cousin Madeleine. There is no need for such anger over one little incident. You must not let it spoil your evening. Look, Miss Wyre is waving to you. Is that her young lord at her side? He is the young gentleman who is to be scratched?'

Madeleine laughed. 'Lord Kilmer is to be brought *up to scratch*, Camille! Lord and Lady Wyre want him to marry Cassandra and he is to be given every opportunity to make her an offer. I think Cassandra wishes to introduce you to him. Come, let us join them. I have every confidence that you will not find his lordship deliberately provoking.'

There was scarcely time for the introductions before the guests were summoned to dinner. Miss Sedgewick found herself seated amongst the London guests. On her immediate right Lord Ragdale addressed himself solely to his food, while Mr Fulbeck on her left showed himself to be an engaging character, but his attention for most of the meal was demanded by the Misses Eldwick, who were sitting in close proximity and could not resist the opportunity of flirting outrageously with their near neighbour. Madeleine was thus at leisure to observe that her cousin, in the company of Miss Wyre and Lord

66

Kilmer at the far end of the table, was suffering no such isolation. Watching their animated conversation, she was aware of a faint pang of envy. This was quickly smothered, although she was forced to stifle a sigh. Looking away, her gaze fell on Mr Hauxwell, sitting at some distance on the opposite side of the table. He was watching her and she blushed slightly, guessing that he had intercepted her envious glance.

* * *

When the ladies retired to the drawing-room, Miss Wyre immediately sought out her friend. Madeleine greeted her with a smile. 'Well, Cassie, I hope you were kind to my cousin.'

'But of course. And he conversed with Kilmer like a sensible man upon any number of topics. He is very taken with you, Maddie, and showed a great interest in you and your family. I think he feels guilty for not making more of a push to stay upon friendly terms with his English relatives.'

'He has no need to do so,' replied Madeleine, frankly. 'It was as much Grandpapa's fault that there was a rift. Poor Camille, his situation is not comfortable.'

'Well, I know Mama and Papa are doing all they can to make him feel welcome. And the

67

other guests too are very affable, are they not? Except, perhaps, that Lord Frederick *is* a little haughty. His wife, too . . . Mama invited them because they are friends of Lord Kilmer — and the Ragdales as well, but I am beginning to wish she had not. Do you see, Lady Frederick and Lady Ragdale are sitting together, yawning behind their fans and making no effort at all to be sociable. Yet when the gentlemen come in you will see a change! They will immediately spring to life, chattering and sparkling and trying to outshine us all. And the Eldwick girls are no better. They have little to say for themselves now, you see.'

'But we, too, are sitting apart,' Madeleine reminded her gently.

'Yes, but we are not doing so out of boredom, are we? Oh, let us forget them, Maddie, and tell me instead what you think of the rest of our guests — Mr Fulbeck, for example.'

'Why, he seemed a pleasant enough gentleman, although we spoke very little over dinner.'

'He is a dreadful flirt, you know.' Cassandra giggled. 'But he cannot help himself. He says it is because he loves all the ladies! And Mr Hauxwell, what do you think of him?'

'Oh I am completely unimpressed.'

'Yet he made you the most flourishing bow.'

'That is *all* it was, mere flourishing. He made no effort to be amiable, and instead went out of his way to be rude to Camille.'

'Really? Yet I thought they would hit it off: Mr Hauxwell is very fond of France, I believe. Papa says he speaks the language like a native.'

'If that is true it is merely so that he may order a new coat,' retorted Miss Sedgewick. 'Apart from learning that he has brought a very handsome horse with him, I have heard nothing to his credit — and I have yet to hear him utter one sensible word.'

Cassandra laughed.

'Oh poor Beau Hauxwell. To have earned such a low opinion. Well, I doubt it will worry him, for there are sufficient ladies here willing to flatter him. And you will see that I am right, for here come the gentlemen now.'

Miss Sedgewick and her friend were in no hurry to conclude their conversation but as Cassandra had prophesied, the entrance of the gentlemen caused a sudden burst of activity amongst most of the ladies. Lady Frederick roused herself sufficiently to be persuaded to open the pianoforte, and soon she and Lady Ragdale were the centre of a lively group. Before Cassandra and Madeleine could join them, they were approached by Mr Fulbeck with Mr Hauxwell at his side.

'Ah, Miss Wyre.' Mr Hauxwell bowed. ''*Like the morn in verdant mantle clad*.' A veritable picture.'

Cassandra blushed and giggled, not knowing how to reply and she looked helplessly at Madeleine.

'Russet,' said Miss Sedgewick.

Beau Hauxwell lifted an eyebrow.

'I beg your pardon?'

'Russet,' she repeated. 'It is '*The morn in russet mantle clad*.' Shakespeare,' she added kindly. 'But of course, since Cassandra is wearing green that would not do, would it? I quite see that.'

The gentleman raised his quizzing glass and regarded her with a fascinated eye. Madeleine put up her chin, returning his look coolly. The quizzing glass was lowered.

'Thank you, ma'am,' he said politely, 'I will endeavour to remember it.'

'I understand, Mr Hauxwell, that you have but recently returned from Paris,' put in Miss Wyre, 'Do you know the country well?'

'Indeed, I like to think so. I have travelled widely on the Continent, but I have a special affection for France.'

'Perhaps you met Miss Sedgewick's cousin

— the Comte du Vivière — while you were there?'

'Alas I did not have that pleasure. However, Sir Thomas introduced us earlier this evening.' His blue eyes swept lazily over Madeleine. 'Perhaps, Miss Sedgewick, you will allow me to say that I can see no family likeness between yourself and the *comte*.'

'It is not obligatory, sir,' she replied shortly.

'No, indeed it is not,' he murmured.

'Miss Wyre,' Mr Fulbeck broke in, 'I have tonight learned that you are proposing to ride out tomorrow, if the weather holds, and I find that Hauxwell here has known of it since his arrival yesterday.'

'No, no, dear friend, it was discussed this morning, over breakfast,' Mr Hauxwell corrected him wearily, 'and if you had been paying a little more attention, Toby, you too would have known of it.'

'Well, I believe it is a deliberate attempt to exclude me from the ride!' declared that gentleman, with mock severity. 'I know your tricks, Andrew. You hoped I should not learn of it until too late, for you are afraid I shall outshine you with the ladies.'

'Alas, my plan is discovered,' sighed Mr. Hauxwell, smiling at Cassandra. 'If we allow Toby to join us, Miss Wyre, I will be obliged to share your company with him as well as

Lord Kilmer. Intolerable! I think, perhaps, I shall not go, after all. We have had such a deal of rain these past weeks, it will be excessively dirty. I think, almost certainly, I shall not go.'

Miss Wyre laughed, a trifle uncertainly, 'How you do joke us, Mr Hauxwell. I am sure we shall all have a splendid day.' She turned to Miss Sedgewick, 'Maddie, do say that you will come, too. You may borrow Snowdrop — she is my second-best mare, you know, and a most beautiful stepper.'

'Thank you, I should like to join you. The pleasure of riding through your father's park is surely worth a little dirt,' she added, with a glance at Mr Hauxwell.

Mr Fulbeck wandered off in search of further amusements, and when Cassandra and Sir Thomas were called away, Madeleine expected Mr Hauxwell to make his excuses and move on. She was disconcerted when he showed no sign of leaving her side.

'The Comte du Vivière is a very fortunate gentleman,' he remarked after a short silence. 'Not every Frenchman can find such support in this country.'

Miss Sedgewick looked surprised.

'I think you do not properly comprehend, sir, how closely the comte is related to my family.'

'Then he is no stranger to you.'

'On the contrary. We have met but once before, as children.' Her eyes travelled across the room to her cousin, who made one of a group of young people gathered about Miss Wyre. 'You are very interested in my cousin, Mr Hauxwell.'

'I like to know as much as possible about a rival, Miss Sedgewick.'

'Then you would be better employed seeking knowledge of Lord Kilmer.'

A glint of a smile touched his lips.

'Since we are all expecting him to offer for Miss Wyre at any time, do you not agree I should be wasting my time in *that* direction?'

'Then who — ' She stopped, feeling very unsure of her ground.

With a bland smile and a graceful bow, the gentleman moved away, leaving her to stare after him in bewilderment.

'I see Mr Hauxwell has been entertaining you, Miss Sedgewick. Do you not find him delightful?' cried Lady Frederick, coming up to her with Lady Ragdale in close attendance.

'I find him an enigma.' admitted Madeleine.

'That is part of his charm,' declared my lady. 'A gentleman of Mr Hauxwell's stature, who can discourse at length upon any subject, who is widely travelled and acclaimed by his friends as a fine sportsman — and yet, he would have us believe that he dislikes all forms of exertion. It hints at a mystery, does it not? Are you not eager to learn more of such a man?'

'Not in the least,' replied Madeleine, affable but blunt. 'I have a liking for sincerity, loyalty and truthfulness. And very little patience with one who puts on such airs which, I strongly suspect, are assumed for the sole purpose of attracting attention.'

Lady Frederick allowed herself a small, contemptuous smile.

'I fear the paragon you seek is to be found only between the covers of a novel, Miss Sedgewick. In reality, I hope you are prepared to settle for something a little less than perfection.'

Upon these words the two ladies moved on, but not before Madeleine heard Lady Frederick's remark to her companion.

'I've no doubt Mr Hauxwell felt a little sorry for her. Such a *tall* girl . . . '

★   ★   ★

With the arrival of the tea tray the small groups that had formed broke up and a more general conversation ensued. Miss Sedgewick soon found Mrs Westlake bearing down upon her and she moved up to make room for her upon the sofa. She smiled in a friendly way, but could not help thinking that Cassie's elder sister lacked her natural warmth and spontaneity. Mrs Westlake sank down upon the sofa.

'Madeleine, my dear friend, at last I have an opportunity to talk with you. How long has it been since we last saw each other; it must be all of twelve months. I vow time passes me by so quickly, especially now, when I am a married woman. It seems such a short while ago that we were at school together, does it not? And yet here I am a veritable matron. Perhaps you have heard' — she lowered her voice and leaned closer — 'Westlake and I are expecting a Happy Event in the summer.'

'How wonderful for you, Jane,' replied Madeleine warmly. 'You must be very happy.'

'Oh I am!' cried Mrs Westlake, 'I never dreamed married life could be so agreeable. But how is it you are still single, Maddie? It cannot be that you lack admirers, I am sure.'

'It is simple. I have not yet met anyone I liked well enough to marry.'

'Well, I would strongly advise you to marry as soon as you can, my dear, for at two-and-twenty a young lady cannot be sure how much longer her looks will last.'

'I confess I had not thought of that,' put in Madeleine, much struck. 'Now I think on it, I do recall seeing a faint wrinkle on my face today. I will have Sarah chop up a cucumber to put upon it — but where *does* one find cucumbers at this season? Will Sir Thomas have some in his hot-house, do you think?'

'I do not think you are taking me seriously, Madeleine.' Mrs Westlake sounded hurt. 'I pray you will consider your situation before it is too late.'

Madeleine struggled to conceal her amusement.

'Indeed I shall, Jane. I will apply my mind to the problem immediately.'

'Good. You will be very grateful to me, one day. Why, even my sister is on the point of a betrothal, that is if she can behave herself long enough for Lord Kilmer to propose.'

'Cassandra appears to think a great deal of his lordship,' remarked Madeleine.

Mrs Westlake gave her a superior smile.

'She is far too complacent about his regard for her. I only hope Mama can impress upon her how necessary it is for a young lady to behave with dignity and propriety, else she will be well served if Kilmer decides to look for a more suitable bride.'

Madeleine could think of nothing to say in reply to these sisterly strictures and she was relieved when Mrs Westlake turned to another subject.

'Oh, there is your cousin, the *comte*. Poor young man. How terrible for him to be a fugitive from his home. One cannot but feel sorry for him.' She gestured to him to approach, 'Monsieur le Comte, has Sir Thomas informed you that you have a compatriot close at hand?'

'No, *madame*, he has not mentioned it.'

'Then I can be the messenger of glad tidings!' declared Mrs Westlake, clapping her hands together. 'I had the news from Parson Dowsett's wife, for I drove over to her this morning — we are such old friends, you know. Well, she tells me that there is a French gentleman come to the village. Of course, there is precious little work about here, especially for a foreigner, but it seems the parson has taken pity upon him and pays him to give French lessons to the children at the church school. I am surprised Papa has not mentioned it to you.'

'I did not see any reason to mention it,' called Sir Thomas, overhearing the remark from across the room. 'He is unlikely to be of interest to our guest. The fellow is merely a clerk or lawyer or some such thing. From Paris.'

'Nevertheless, to have a countryman so near excites my interest,' remarked the *comte*.

'I daresay he would be delighted to meet

you,' put in Mrs Westlake encouragingly. 'Why do you not call on him, Comte?'

'I should not care to impose myself, but I could, perhaps, write to him a brief note?'

'The very thing,' cried Mrs Westlake, ignoring her father's frown. 'The poor man and his wife have lodgings in West Street, with old Mrs Hodges. I am sure he would be grateful for your interest.'

'Thank you, *madame*,' the *comte* bowed. 'Although I fear my interest will be of little use to him at present.'

A servant came in carrying a sealed letter on a tray. After a brief word with Sir Thomas, he presented the missive to Mr Sedgewick, who broke the seal and spread open the sheet, the paper crackling loudly in the expectant silence that had fallen over the room.

'Is the messenger still here?' he asked, without looking up.

'He is in the hall, sir. He says he has come direct from Stapley.'

'See if you can find him some food and, with Sir Thomas's permission, a bed for the night. Tell him I'll ride back to Town with him in the morning.'

Sir Thomas nodded to the footman, but said nothing until the servant had left the room.

'Trouble, George?'

'It is from Grenville. I must return to Town in the morning.'

Murmurs of apprehension ran around the room.

'So soon?' cried Lady Wyre, 'but, my dear sir, you have only just arrived!'

'I know, ma'am, and I regret the necessity of it,' he answered her sadly. 'However, had this message come a day earlier I should have had to cry off altogether. As it is I have spent a most enjoyable day here.'

'Are we at war, Papa?' Madeleine asked quietly.

'Very close to it, my dear. Antwerp has fallen. There's very little hope that peace can be preserved now. The militia are being called out and Parliament is to meet again in a fortnight.'

'Well, all I can say is thank Heaven something is being done at last!' declared Mr Eldwick, his eyes blazing fiercely in his bewhiskered face. 'We've been shilly-shallying far too long — all these mutterings of war are most unsettling. Let us be up and at 'em, the sooner the better, is what I say!'

With embarrassed glances towards the Comte du Vivière, his daughters blushed and murmured their incoherent protests at his belligerence. Madeleine went to her father's side.

'Should Mama and I return to Stapley, Papa?'

'What's that, Maddie? No, no, I see no need for you to curtail your stay here, unless your mama is desirous to be at home.' He looked enquiringly at his wife, who shook her head so emphatically that her carefully set ringlets danced around her head.

'If our hosts do not object, I would prefer to remain here,' she said, not wishing to come within range of Sir Joseph's uncertain temper without her husband's supportive presence.

'Of course you must stay!' cried Lady Wyre. 'I will not hear another word about your leaving. You will be far better off remaining here, with your friends.'

Mrs Sedgewick looked relieved and her husband nodded.

'I am in agreement with you, Lady Wyre. We have had scares like this one before — it might well blow over and I could be back here again in a week or so.'

The news had cast a cloud over the evening, and very soon the party broke up, Mr Sedgewick retiring to prepare for an early start, the others hoping that with a night's repose they could banish the gloomy tidings to the background, at least for a while.

6

Madeleine rose before dawn the following morning in order to bid her father goodbye. Sir Thomas had put one of his carriages at his guest's disposal, to convey him to Town in a much shorter time than the Sedgewicks' old travelling coach could ever hope to achieve. Madeleine found her father in the hall, donning a thick cloak to ward off the cold. Her mother, wrapped in a trailing shawl, hovered around him, her countenance anxious and drawn. Mr Sedgewick took his leave of them, and with a reassuring smile and a word to Madeleine to look after her mama, he stepped up into the carriage and was soon moving swiftly away down the drive as the first grey fingers of light were pushing back the night clouds.

They watched until the carriage was out of sight, then Mrs Sedgewick declared with a shiver that she was returning to her bed. Madeleine made her way back up the stairs to her own chamber, but she was filled with a strange restlessness and knew she would not sleep again that morning. Upon a sudden impulse, she put on a pair of stout walking boots, sought out her warmest pelisse and left her room, much to the amazement of the young maid who had only just arrived to make up the fire there. From her frequent visits to Wyre as a child, Madeleine was familiar with the building and she ignored the main doors, preferring to make her way downstairs to slip out through a side door in the rustic, on the east side of the house. It was still only half-light, and she hesitated for a moment before setting off in a southerly direction. Her route took her through the open parkland that surrounded the house and flower-gardens, and on towards the woods she had so often explored with Jane and Cassandra during their youthful adventures. She had no intention of entering them now — the morning light was not yet strong enough to pierce the gloom of the closely packed trees, where the mournful cry of rooks was the only sign of life. Instead she turned westward and walked along a track that bordered the edge of the woods. The air was fresh but there was no frost and Madeleine found her fur-lined coat almost too warm for her exertions. She slackened her pace a little, enjoying the solitude. She was thinking ruefully that the wet would soon be penetrating her boots when a movement a short distance ahead of her caught her attention. As she watched, a tall figure dressed in a plain brown coat, buckskins and riding boots emerged from the trees. She was startled to recognize Mr Hauxwell. He, on the other hand, showed not the slightest surprise upon seeing her but merely stopped, one hand resting lightly upon his silver-topped cane, and waited for her to come up to him.

'Good morning, Miss Sedgewick — *'Like Phoebe from her chamber of the east'*,' he quoted, bowing.

Despite her irritation with the gentleman the previous evening, Madeleine laughed.

'I am glad you did not add the next part — *'with portly pace'* — for it is impossible to be majestic when one's heels are gripped by mud!'

Turning to walk beside her, he offered his arm and after the briefest hesitation, she put up her hand, realizing it would be churlish to refuse.

'You know Spenser, ma'am?'

'I read his work avidly in my schooldays — though pray do not think that I am bookish,' she added, remembering Cassandra's words. 'It merely chanced that you chose lines I remember well. I am surprised that you can quote so freely this early in the day. I had thought gentlemen of fashion kept to their rooms until noon at least!'

'A headache,' he explained. 'I was in the greatest discomfort hours before the dawn and at length I decided upon a little exercise to try if that would clear my head. I would not for the world mention it to Sir Thomas' — he dropped his voice conspiratorially — 'I suspect it was the brandy.'

'So you have been walking — and in this mud too!'

'You are doubtless recalling my comment last night,' he replied, her gentle irony not lost upon him. 'Then I was referring to riding, Miss Sedgewick. To go out alone for a walk is quite another thing, for then one can exercise a certain degree of care, and there is no one to observe the odd stain. I must tell you, ma'am, how much it distresses me to have you find me thus! I vow there is even a speck of mud upon my sleeve — I am mortified.'

'You need have no fear, sir, I do not regard it, and I shall not mention the matter to a soul,' she assured him. Her tone was cool and faintly contemptuous, but he appeared not to notice. He stopped and stepped back to make her an elegant bow.

'I am your most devoted servant, ma'am. It is not often one meets with such sympathy, such a true understanding of what one is suffering.'

'To be truthful, I find your concern over such a trifling matter quite incomprehensible,' she remarked acidly. 'Pray let us continue, or it will take us forever to reach the house!'

'As you wish, Miss Sedgewick.'

He uttered the words meekly, but something in his tone made her look up at him suspiciously. He returned her gaze with a bland look of enquiry and, ignoring the proffered arm, she strode away, having the distinct impression that he was laughing at her. Mr Hauxwell soon caught up with her and they walked on in silence. Soon they reached a fork in the track and turned their backs to the woods as they headed towards the house.

'Your father has this morning left for London, Miss Sedgewick? Do you know when he expects to return?'

'He could not say. It depends very much upon the situation in France, I believe.'

'No doubt he is heavily involved in affairs of state.'

She looked up, surprised.

'No, although at one time he had hoped — but with the untimely death of my uncle last year, Papa became heir to Stapley and he sees it as his duty to take up his responsibilites there. He has already said that he would retire from government circles completely, if we had a more stable peace. However, he maintains that it is every true Englishman's duty to support the government at the present time.'

'No doubt your cousin's plight has brought home to you the terrible predicament that now affects France.'

'Yes, indeed. I was used to follow developments there with an almost detached interest, but now it all seems so much more real, and I am appalled by what I hear. How can people be so — so implacable, to execute dozens — no, hundreds — of men and women, because they are loyal to their king!'

'You must remember that many have also died because they hated him,' he reminded her.

'Do you know France well, sir? Whenever you speak of that country it is with affection.'

'I hold the country in *great* affection, Miss Sedgewick.'

She frowned slightly. 'I find it unusual that you did not take more time to discuss France with my cousin.'

He gave a soft laugh. 'I fear perhaps our views on some points would differ greatly. By the by, does the *comte* ride out with you today?'

'No. He made his apologies to Sir Thomas

last night. I think it was the news of the worsening situation between England and France — he cannot help but be affected, do you not agree?' she looked up at him, her enquiring hazel eyes meeting thoughtful blue ones.

'Oh undoubtedly, Miss Sedgewick, undoubtedly. The *comte*'s command of our language is excellent, is it not? No doubt he has been a frequent visitor to England?'

She shook her head. 'Why no. I do not believe he has been here since we were children — at least, he may have come to England without informing us. His last visit to Stapley ended in a blazing row between the old *comte* and my grandfather, so it is possible he did not wish to pursue the connection, until now.'

'Yes. Until now.' He raised his cane and pointed to a flight of stone steps that led up to the terrace on the south front of Wyre Hall. 'Do you wish to enter that way?'

'I would suggest it would be simpler if we continue up to the house. I can enter by one of the lower side doors. They are sure to be unlocked by this time and even if they are not, I can always go around to the east front, for I left a side door unlocked there when I came out. No doubt you did the same when you left your apartments — you are in the west wing, I suppose? I thought as much: it was built expressly for guests.'

'And thus ends a most enjoyable interlude,' he murmured, as they walked past the sheltering bank and hedge separating them from the formal gardens.

They were soon treading on the wide gravel path along the side of the house itself. As she had foreseen, a side door opened easily, but she paused and turned back before going in, as though there was something else to be said before parting. Her companion provided a quotation.

''And wilt thou leave me thus? Say nay, for shame!'.'

Her eyes danced with sudden merriment.

'I can match you there, sir — *'I have done: you get no more of me'.'*

'Well done, Miss Sedgewick,' he smiled approvingly, 'but perhaps you do not recall the first line of that poem: *'Come, let us kiss and part'.'*

For one frightening moment she thought he would suit the action to the words and with a hurried farewell she whisked herself inside and closed the door, leaning back against it and listening until the crunch of footsteps on the gravel told her that the gentleman had gone. She remained by the door, feeling strangely exhilarated. What an odd person he was, to be sure. She had thought she disliked him, but now she knew not what to think. During their walk he had kept her well entertained and for the most part without the faintly foppish behaviour she had observed on the previous evening. Why he should wish to appear so affected in public she had no idea, but she would not allow the matter to worry her for, she told herself firmly, it was really none of her concern. After several minutes, Madeleine became aware of her surroundings. She was in a small vestibule leading on one side to Sir Thomas's study and on the other to the billiard-room: she would need to traverse one or the other of these apartments to reach the stairs, but she had no wish to leave a trail of muddy footprints through either. After the briefest hesitation, she unlaced her boots and took them off, then she slipped quickly through the billiard-room and up the stairs to the main floor. She could hear the servants going about their work in the main hall and the breakfast-room, but there was no one on the stairs. Madeleine was beginning to hope that she would reach the safety of her bedchamber unobserved when voices from the landing informed her that Lady Wyre and her daughter were approaching. She reached the head of the stairs just as they appeared, and

Lady Wyre raised her brows as she spotted Miss Sedgewick, eyes bright, cheeks glowing and a pair of extremely muddy half-boots clutched in one hand.

'Maddie, we are just going down to breakfast!' declared Cassandra, staring at her friend. 'Where have you been, so early in the day?'

Their shocked faces very nearly overset Madeleine, but she managed to say she had been walking, before breaking into a peal of laughter as she sped past them and on to her own room.

★　★　★

Some thirty minutes later, Miss Sedgewick came down to the breakfast-room, neat as a pin and showing no signs of her early morning exertions except the added glow in her hazel eyes. There was a great deal of bustling activity in the room and an almost festive atmosphere, as if all the guests were determined to enjoy themselves. Madeleine quickly surveyed the assembly: Cassandra, with Lord Kilmer in close attendance, was standing at a side table deep in conversation; Mrs Westlake was absent, and Madeleine guessed that Jane's delicate condition was the reason for this. Camille was also missing, as was Mr Hauxwell.

Sir Thomas beckoned Madeleine to an empty place beside him, saying as she took her seat, 'Like a dashed Welsh fair, so many people! Never saw such a crowd here before, but there it is, if it makes my ladies happy, I can live with it — for a while. Can't pretend I'll be sorry to see the end o' the week, for then half of 'em will be off.'

'Oh, how is that? I understood everyone would be staying until the New Year, sir.'

Sir Thomas shook his head. 'No, no, the Ragdales, Martons and their party are going on with Lord Frederick to his place in Leicestershire. They'll be off at the end of the week, after the ball. I hope you have brought your very best gown, Maddie. My lady is determined it is to be a sparkling affair.'

'I have something that will suffice, sir. Cassandra told me she had persuaded you to give a little party.'

'Lord love you, Cassie plagued my life to have some kind of merry-making, so I agreed to it. Heaven knows why I indulge her so.'

'Because you are an excellent father,' replied Madeleine boldly. 'I have known you too long to be taken in by your talk, Sir Thomas. You delight in making people happy and I know you enjoy a party as much as anyone.'

91

He chuckled. 'Aye, you're a clever little puss, and I'm always happy to have you at Wyre, Maddie. Come, let me recommend the ham to you. It is from our Home Farm you know, and it is exceptionally good.'

'Thank you. Do you ride with us this morning, Sir Thomas?'

'Aye, m'dear. My lady and I are going along to keep you young folk in some sort of order.' He turned to Mrs Eldwick, sitting on his right, 'You should come too, ma'am. We could find you a nice steady mount. It would do you good, I've no doubt.'

'Heavens, Sir Thomas. You do not know what you are saying!' cried that lady, all a-flutter, 'My health could never permit such a thing.'

'Pho, a gentle ride across the park could do no harm,' he coaxed, but Mrs Eldwick shook her head.

'My dear sir, I do not believe you understand. You have never suffered from a moment's illness in your life, I am sure, but my constitution is not at all robust. No, I must leave my dear girls in your charge and Mr Eldwick shall take me for a quiet drive in an open carriage later in the day, if the weather remains fine. I trust that if I am well wrapped and have a hot brick to place beneath my feet, I shall be safe enough.'

Sir Thomas turned back to Madeleine with a sigh.

'Never met with such a set for staying indoors,' he told her, between mouthfuls of ham. 'Lord Frederick has sent his own hunters on to Leicestershire and is disinclined to ride any others, and the rest of his crowd have no desire to go without him — I dare swear there will be less than a dozen of us riding out this morning.'

With a sympathetic murmur, Miss Sedgewick settled down to her breakfast and was just putting down her empty coffee cup when Cassandra approached her.

'Are you finished here, Maddie? If you are going upstairs, I shall go with you.'

Madeleine was quick to note her troubled countenance and rose immediately.

'Yes, of course. I am quite done, let us go at once.'

As the door of the breakfast-room closed behind them, Madeleine lost no time in demanding that her friend should tell her what was amiss.

'Everything!' was the dramatic reply.

Before she could explain, they heard voices and very soon Mr Hauxwell appeared at the turn of the stairs, leaning upon the arm of Mr Fulbeck. Too agitated to speak, Miss Wyre hurried up the stairs with Madeleine close behind her and the gentlemen stopped on the half-landing to allow the ladies to pass with only the briefest of acknowledgements. Observing Mr Hauxwell's blue velvet coat, white waistcoat and canary knee-breeches, Madeleine was aware of an irrational disappointment.

'So he really does mean to remain indoors,' she murmured.

'Who — Mr Hauxwell? I am sure I do not care,' replied Cassandra in a petulant tone.

'My dear Cassie, what has happened to put you in such a bad skin?'

'Kilmer! He has been so — so *odious* to me, there is no bearing it.'

'No, no, I cannot believe it,' said Madeleine soothingly. 'Why, he is such a — a quiet gentleman.'

Miss Wyre drew a deep breath and said in a low voice, 'He had the — the audacity to — to forbid me to dance twice with any other gentleman at Thursday's ball!'

She looked so indignant that Miss Sedgewick was tempted to laugh. She controlled the impulse and said calmly, 'Now why should he do that? Are you sure you did not provoke him?'

'I merely told him that I *might* do so, just to tease him a little, but he was so cross and it ended with his ordering me to dance not more than once with any gentlemen but himself. I was never more outraged. He has no right to tell me what to do, we are not even engaged. Why do you laugh at me, Maddie? I felt sure you would understand.'

'Oh, I do,' replied her friend, chuckling. 'You set out to vex him and succeeded only too well. I think you would do well to heed Lord Kilmer, if you are serious about him, Cassie. He is not a — a frivolous young man and it will not do to try his patience too far, I think.'

Miss Wyre hunched a shoulder.

'I am sure I do not care. I will not be ordered around in such a way. I shall dance with anyone I choose on Thursday — and as many times as I wish, too!'

Realizing it would be futile to argue, Miss Sedgewick held her peace, hoping that the forthcoming ride would drive away Cassandra's crotchets.

★　★　★

The riding party set out shortly before noon and it was soon apparent to Sir Thomas that the young people needed no curb on their high spirits. The Misses Eldwick and Miss Marton were nervous riders who enjoyed nothing faster than a gentle canter. Mr

Edward Marton, no doubt a clipping rider to the hounds, was showing a marked attachment to Miss Phoebe Eldwick and was thus content to ride quietly at her side. His goddaughter he knew to be an excellent rider, and although she might find the party a little slow, she was a sensible girl and he was sure she would happily fall in with the crowd. No, mused Sir Thomas, the only member of the party to cause him concern was Cassandra, who was riding beside Mr Fulbeck. He was well aware that his daughter had joined the ride in a less than sunny mood and suspected she had fallen out with Lord Kilmer. However, he was hopeful that the combination of a good gallop and Mr Fulbeck's considerable powers of address would bring her out of the sullens. The fellow was a rattle, to be sure, but Sir Thomas was confident that he would not let Cassandra come to any harm. Lord Kilmer, riding some distance behind Miss Wyre and her companion, would have found little comfort in this reassurance. His face as he watched Cassandra was unnaturally grim and observing this, Madeleine was prompted to ride up beside his lordship.

'Miss Wyre is looking very well today, my lord.'

'Indeed — perfect in looks, perhaps, but as to temperament . . . '

He stopped, obviously labouring under some intense emotion. Madeleine said gently, 'Cassandra is a very high-spirited young lady, sir. I have no doubt that she sometimes allows her temper to override her judgement.'

Lord Kilmer laughed harshly. 'Well put, Miss Sedgewick. I fear I have been mistaken in the lady.'

'Oh I doubt it, sir. She is very young and has some very — how shall we say it? — romantic notions.'

'Doubtless she would like me to carry her off to Gretna. No, ma'am. I demand more becoming conduct from the future Lady Kilmer.'

'I would hazard a guess that you have not yet told her of your affection for her, sir.'

He flushed. 'Of course not. Why, I have not yet spoken to Sir Thomas.'

'Would you have me believe he has no notion of your intentions?'

'He has been most amiable, and obliging — '

'But you expect your offer to be received favourably.'

'I do not think Sir Thomas will find my proposal contemptible,' he returned, with cool dignity.

'And you expect Cassie to sit by placidly waiting for you to act? No doubt it was her docility that first attracted you.'

The irony was not lost upon Lord Kilmer. He smiled reluctantly.

'Very well, Miss Sedgewick, I take your point.' He looked again towards Miss Wyre, who was laughing now at some remark of Mr Fulbeck's and his jaw tightened. 'But if she cared for me — '

'She *does* care for you!' Madeleine assured him. 'What she does not know is whether you return her regard, or if you are looking upon her as some sort of possession. Consider, sir, how you may best proceed.' She said no more and dropped back to ride beside Lady Wyre, hoping that the thoughtful look on his lordship's countenance meant he would heed her words, and perhaps act upon them. She was pleased to see him riding alongside Cassandra soon after and Madeleine hoped she had been of some use.

The party had turned for home and were re-entering the park when a lone rider was seen approaching. When he saw them, he waved and cantered across to join them.

'By Jove, it's the young Frenchman!' declared Sir Thomas. 'Ah, *comte*! So glad you decided to get out of the house. Why did you not join us?'

'I have been searching for you,' explained Camille as he drew alongside. 'One of your stable boys said you had gone north. It has taken me so long to find you.' He fell in beside Madeleine. 'You have had an enjoyable day, *non?*'

'Yes I have, thank you. Have you been searching for us a very long time?'

He shrugged. 'An hour, perhaps more. I am not sure how long . . .'

'Judging by the state of you, you have had a lively ride!' she laughed, looking at the generous splashing of mud over horse and rider. They were in sight of the house and very soon the party was clattering into the stable yard. Miss Sedgewick's attention was caught by the sight of a big black hunter that was being led across the yard. 'Oh, what a beautiful creature!'

'Oh, that's Jove, Mr Hauxwell's horse,' explained Cassandra, drawing up beside her, 'I daresay the groom has been exercising him.'

'I saw you talking to Lord Kilmer,' ventured Madeleine. 'Have you resolved your differences now?'

'Of course. He apologized to me most handsomely, so now we are the best of friends again.'

'He apologized!' cried Miss Sedgewick in surprise. 'I would have thought, from what you told me, that your own behaviour was far from perfect.'

'Oh he is far too infatuated with me to worry about that,' came the unconcerned reply. 'I told Mama as much when he arrived here and his apology today proves it, does it not?'

Madeleine did not agree, but she said nothing and in high good humour Cassandra accompanied her friend upstairs. They parted on the landing and Madeleine was looking forward to a quiet hour before preparing for dinner. She was a little surprised to find her maid absent from her room. She was anxious to change out of her muddy habit and she tugged at the bell-rope impatiently.

'Sarah, where have you been!' she demanded, when the girl came hurrying in.

'Oh, miss, such a thing,' cried Sarah, her cheeks very flushed. 'There's been a murder!'

7

Hurriedly changing into a clean gown, Miss Sedgewick made her way to the drawing-room, where she found Lady Wyre and most of her guests gathered together.

'Madeleine, have you heard the dreadful news?' cried Mrs Sedgewick, seated beside her hostess.

'My maid has given me something of the tale, but it was so jumbled I was hoping you could enlighten me.' Madeleine looked anxiously towards Lady Wyre.

'It is the Frenchman,' cried Mrs Westlake. 'He has been most foully murdered!' She lay back upon the sofa, her vinaigrette in her hand.

Madeleine cast a puzzled look towards her cousin.

'No, no, Maddie, it has nothing to do with Monsieur le Comte,' Lady Wyre hastened to reassure her. 'Jane is speaking of the French lawyer, Monsieur Breton, who lived in the village.'

'Yes!' cried Mrs Westlake, sitting up again. 'Brutally done to death, and so close — I do not believe I shall ever recover — '

'You were there?' asked Miss Sedgewick, startled.

Jane shook her head. 'I was visiting Mrs Dowsett at the parsonage. It was such a beautiful day and as I could not ride, I thought a gentle drive could do no harm. How little did I guess then — ' She broke off, reviving herself with her vinaigrette before continuing. 'We were enjoying such a comfortable coze, when in burst Mr Dowsett, looking greatly agitated, and saying Mrs Dowsett must go immediately to Mrs Hodges' house. Of course we demanded to know what had occurred and when I heard, I offered to go with Mrs Dowsett. You may imagine that Mrs Hodges was quite overset, and Madame Breton — to be widowed so cruelly in a foreign land.'

'You would have done better to come home, Jane,' remarked Lady Wyre, frowning. 'This upset will do you no good in your present condition.'

'But, Mama, I could not leave without knowing if I could be of use, and by taking Mrs Dowsett to the village, Parson was free to go with Mr Hauxwell to the magistrate.'

'Excuse me, *madame*, you say Mr Hauxwell was present?' queried Camille.

Mrs Westlake opened her eyes very wide. 'Why yes! Did I not tell you that it was he who discovered the body? He is even now closeted with Papa.'

'Jane, dearest, will you not go to your room and lie down,' begged Mr Westlake, looking anxiously at his wife's pale face.

'Oh no, I could not bear to be alone!' she declared, clinging to his hand. 'When I think of that poor woman — her command of the language is not great, you know, and Mrs Hodges is in no state to aid her, for she had already taken to her bed, after being disturbed by intruders just before dawn this morning.'

'Good heavens!' cried Mrs Sedgewick. 'I trust no one was hurt?'

'No indeed, for the dogs raised the alarm, and whoever it was ran off, but it must have been very unsettling — '

She broke off as the door opened to admit Sir Thomas, accompanied by Mr Hauxwell.

'Ah, my dear Sir Thomas, here's some dark times upon us,' Mrs Eldwick greeted him gloomily.

'Dark indeed, ma'am,' agreed her host, shaking his head. He turned towards his eldest daughter, 'Jane, my dear, should you not be in your room? You have been through a great deal today.'

'Yes, sir, do try to persuade her to lie

down,' put in Mr Westlake. 'She will not listen to me, but I cannot like her tiring herself so.' His wife sighed and struggled to sit up once more.

'Very well, if you will give me your arm, Mr Westlake, I will retire,' she capitulated, rising slowly to her feet. 'I doubt I could sit through dinner, in any event. Just a little thin soup sent to my room, Mama, and I shall do very well, but someone must stay with me, I will not be alone!'

'You are safe enough, my love, but we will have one of the maids remain with you at all times, so that you may rest easy . . . '

There was a sympathetic silence as Mr Westlake gently escorted his lady from the room.

'Poor little thing. I doubt she will sleep much tonight,' said Mr Eldwick, shaking his head.

'No more will that poor French widow-woman,' added Sir Thomas.

'Do you have any clue as to the murderer?' asked Lord Frederick.

Sir Thomas shook his head. 'No, nothing yet.'

'But who would want to do such a thing?' demanded Lady Wyre, 'What could anyone hope to gain from killing the poor man?'

'There is a deal of anti-French feeling in

the country at present, ma'am,' put in Mr Hauxwell.

Madeleine looked instinctively towards her cousin.

'It could happen again,' she murmured, almost to herself.

'Not at Wyre Hall,' put in Sir Thomas with great firmness. 'I shall instruct the servants to take extra care when locking up at night, and have a couple of my fellows check the grounds every evening. I'll not have my guests murdered in their beds, never fear!'

★   ★   ★

Dinner was a subdued affair, as was to be expected and the gentlemen did not remain long in the dining-room but soon joined the ladies, well before the tea tray appeared. Talk of the day's events was not to be avoided, and Mrs Eldwick was so ill at ease that Sir Thomas somewhat testily offered to have a servant posted at her door all night, if it would make her rest easier.

'Oh hush, Mama,' begged Miss Eldwick. 'There can be no danger to *you*, after all.'

'Of course not,' agreed Mr Eldwick. 'I am much inclined to think that it was an isolated incident, and a cowardly one at

105

that, to attack a poor schoolteacher. What do you say, Hauxwell?'

That gentleman closed his eyes and shuddered visibly.

'I try not to think of it at all. The whole affair has left me with a disinclination to venture out alone.'

'And what is to be done for poor Madame Breton?' enquired Mrs Sedgewick.

'I will call upon her tomorrow,' replied Sir Thomas, 'to ensure that she is not wanting for anything.'

'Poor woman,' sighed Lady Wyre. 'I have a mind to come with you, Sir Thomas, for I am sure she must be feeling her loss most wretchedly. I might perhaps be some comfort to her.'

'I believe Mrs Dowsett has taken her to the parsonage, so she is in good hands, m'dear.'

The Comte du Vivière stepped forward.

'It would please me if you would take this to her,' he said, drawing from his hand a large ruby ring. 'I believe it is quite valuable. Naturally I cannot say how much it might be sold for — '

'Camille, my dear boy!' cried Mrs Sedgewick. 'That ring is a family heirloom! Is it not the very one your dear mama took with her from England when she married the old *comte*?'

For a brief second Camille hesitated, then he smiled slightly.

'I have little need for heirlooms now, dear ma'am. It is better put to some use.'

He handed it to Sir Thomas, who cried, 'Why that's most generous of you, sir! Very generous, I am sure. Madame Breton will be most grateful when I tell her — '

'No, no, I would prefer that you do not mention me,' said the *comte* quickly.

'Very well, if that is what you wish.'

The *comte* bowed slightly and moved off and Miss Sedgewick followed him.

'Forgive me, Cousin, but I must tell you how I am moved by your generosity. To give away your ring, when you have so little of your own — such unselfishness quite humbles me!'

He took her hand and raised it briefly to his lips.

'Your esteem is all the wealth I require, Madeleine,' he said softly. 'I wish I had the right to ask for more, but in my present position . . . '

Madeleine gently drew her hand away.

'Please, Camille, you must not talk so.'

She noticed that Mr Hauxwell was standing close by, observing them.

'I know I have not the right to speak, Cousin, but perhaps one day.'

'Perhaps.' She smiled fleetingly before moving away, passing Mr Hauxwell without meeting his eyes.

That gentleman strolled over to the *comte*.

'It has been an eventful day, *m'sieur*, would you not agree?'

'A very unpleasant one, for some of us, sir.'

'The poor fellow was a lawyer, I understand,' continued Mr Hauxwell smoothly. 'A profession not unknown in your own family, I believe.'

The Comte du Vivière looked blank.

'Your own cousin is a lawyer in Paris, is he not?'

'Ah, yes. I believe he is,' replied Camille indifferently. 'I have had little to do with him in recent years. You are acquainted with him, perhaps?'

'No, no, but I have heard of Monsieur Menotte. He is making quite a name for himself in Paris.'

'Then you have the advantage of me, *m'sieur*. I know very little of my cousin Eugène. Our lives run very separate courses now.'

'As if he never existed, perhaps?'

Camille laughed softly. 'What an odd expression, Mr Hauxwell. My cousin would take exception to it, I am sure.'

The gentleman inclined his head.

'I hope one day to have the pleasure of meeting him,' he murmured, then, with a faint smile, he moved off.

★ ★ ★

For much of the evening Miss Wyre was at the centre of a group of lively young people, engaged in light-hearted conversation with much joking and laughter, but towards the end of the evening she broke away and went in search of Miss Sedgewick.

'Maddie, have you seen Kilmer?'

'He went off with Mr Westlake to play billiards. You look anxious, Cassie. Have you quarrelled again?'

'No, nothing like that,' she replied, the crease between her brows deepening, 'I have not seen a great deal of him tonight and he has been — oh, I do not know — distant, I suppose you might say.'

Miss Sedgewick smiled faintly. 'Are you afraid of losing him, Cassie?'

'No, of course not! It is merely that I am — concerned. He is usually so attentive.'

Miss Sedgewick hesitated, then said slowly, 'If you will let me offer you some advice, Cassie. Try if *you* can be a little more *attentive* towards his lordship. I fear the poor gentleman is none too certain of your regard for him.'

109

Miss Wyre pouted. 'Oh, don't lecture me, Maddie, if you please. Kilmer is besotted with me.'

'Not so besotted that he will let you ride roughshod over him for ever,' replied her friend bluntly. 'Try to consider his feelings, or you may well lose him.

'I shall not listen to you, for you do not understand,' said Cassandra petulantly. 'I am very tired: I think I shall go to bed.'

Madeleine watched her friend depart, a frown in her own clear eyes, and when she turned, she found her cousin at her side.

'Mademoiselle Wyre is out of spirits?' he asked lightly.

'I am afraid I gave her some advice that she found unpalatable.' Madeleine sighed. 'Mayhap I am wrong, but I have no wish for her to be unhappy.'

'She has every advantage: good family, beauty and a not inconsiderable fortune. How can she fail to be happy?'

'I think that so many advantages have made her a little . . . wilful,' replied Miss Sedgewick wryly.

'She is but a child,' he observed. 'She has a lot to learn. For myself, I prefer someone with a little more *bon sens*.' His speaking look brought the colour flooding her cheeks and she turned away, reluctant to pursue that line of thought.

'Today's tragic events have quelled our spirits,' she remarked. 'We are all very quiet tonight.'

The *comte* agreed and after a brief pause, he said, 'What do you know of Mr Hauxwell?'

'Very little. He is an acquaintance of Sir Thomas, I believe, although he is not a close friend of the family. Why do you ask?'

He shrugged. 'Oh, it is merely a suspicion that I have that the gentleman dislikes me — perhaps because I am French.'

'Oh surely not! Why, I have heard him say he is very fond of your country!'

'That is not quite the same thing as liking its people,' he replied. 'I regret that I am distrustful of the gentleman. He would have us think him a — how do you say it? — a fop, but I think perhaps it hides a more sinister character.'

Madeleine laughed. 'I cannot believe it! You are allowing your fancy to run away with you, Cousin.'

'Am I? Where was Mr Hauxwell when my countryman was so callously murdered, I wonder?'

'It was he who discovered the body.'

'That is what we have been told, but perhaps that is not all the truth. Do we know why the gentleman was in that area?'

Madeleine shook her head disbelievingly.

'No, no you are jumping at shadows, Cousin. Mr Hauxwell would not . . . ' she trailed off into silence.

'Go on, Madeleine, what thought has occurred to you?'

'It — it is only conjecture,' she murmured, 'most likely it has nothing to do with the matter, but I *saw* Mr Hauxwell this morning, coming out of the South Wood.'

The *comte* was very attentive. His dark eyes were fixed on her face.

'Carry on, if you please.'

'It was early, just growing light and I met him in the park. He said he had been walking in the woods.'

'You saw only him?'

'Yes. I am quite sure there was no one else in the park at that time in the morning.'

Camille looked grave. 'Did they not say that Mrs Hodges had been disturbed this morning by an intruder?'

She cast an anguished look at him. 'No. It cannot be!' she whispered. 'Mr Hauxwell walked back to the house with me — he was so pleasant, and completely at ease. It is too incredible. You must be mistaken.'

'A man who can shoot another in the back is unlikely to betray himself so easily.'

112

Miss Sedgewick looked across the room at Mr Hauxwell, standing at his ease and conversing with Mr Fulbeck.

'Then, you could be in danger, Camille,' she said, scarcely above a whisper.

'That is very probable,' he agreed. 'Cousin, we must be very careful. I want you to be very brave for me, and act as if we had said nothing of this.'

'I wish nothing *had* been said!'

'Will you help me, Cousin?'

Madeleine stared into his face for a long moment before answering.

'Of course, Camille.'

'Then I would like you to help me watch this Mr Hauxwell. Tell me of anything strange or suspicious that might occur.'

'Of course, but would it not be better to lay the whole before Sir Thomas — '

'By no means!' he said emphatically. 'If our suspicions are correct, this man is very dangerous — and clever, also. We must be sure of ourselves before we act. It is also possible that he will try to throw some suspicion upon me.'

'He has already asked me a number of questions concerning you,' admitted Madeleine. She cast another quick glance across the room. 'I cannot believe it. It is like a bad dream.'

'Courage, *ma chère*. It is courage will win the day.'

There was no time for more. Lady Wyre approached, to demand Miss Sedgewick's services at the pianoforte.

'The Eldwick girls wish to sing for us,' she explained, 'but neither of them can play without music and they say they must have accompaniment.'

It was near midnight when the party broke up and Miss Sedgewick was only too glad to reach the seclusion of her bedchamber, where she allowed the chaotic jumble of her thoughts to run freely through her mind. She could not believe her cousin's suspicions, yet neither could she totally dismiss them, and she was still trying to put her tangled thoughts into some sort of order when she fell asleep.

★ ★ ★

She rose the next morning feeling little refreshed from her night's repose and went down to breakfast in a very thoughtful mood. She was greeted warmly by Sir Thomas and his lady and chose a vacant seat close to them. Sitting opposite was Mr Hauxwell, but she knew not how to return his smile and quickly looked away, pretending she had not seen it. She turned her attention to Lady Wyre, who was speaking.

'Cassandra is still in her room. She is complaining of the headache, but I think it is too much excitement. I am hopeful that if she rests quietly this morning her spirits will recover. Most of the other young people are in the music-room, practising their dancing for the ball tomorrow night. I understand Mr Fulbeck is showing them some of the latest steps — even Monsieur le Comte has been persuaded to join in.' She saw her husband's alarmed countenance and added soothingly, 'The Martons are also advising them, my dear sir, so you need have no fear that their high spirits will lead to mischief.'

'I suppose Lord Frederick and the Ragdales are not yet out of their rooms,' replied her spouse, chuckling. 'Never known a set like it for keeping to their beds. They miss the best part of the day, so they do!'

'For myself, I wish I could sleep more,' put in Mrs Eldwick in a complaining tone. 'The sad fact is that as soon as I wake up, I must *get* up, or suffer an aching head for the rest of the day. Mr Eldwick knows how it is, do you not, sir? He is forever telling me I should rest more, but no, I say, it is not in my nature to be idle, I must be busy.'

Miss Sedgewick exchanged a humorous

glance with her hostess as the lady continued to list the various ailments that afflicted her, and as the monologue continued uninterrupted and largely unheeded, Madeleine gave her attention to her breakfast.

'You are going to the village this morning, Sir Thomas, are you not?' enquired Mr Westlake, when at last Mrs Eldwick had temporarily exhausted her subject.

'Aye, my lady and I are going to see what can be done for the poor French widow. We shall call at the parsonage to discover how she goes on.'

'Jane wanted to go with you, but yesterday's events have overset her so much that I have persuaded her to remain in her room,' explained Mr Westlake, shaking his head. 'She is in no condition to be jauntering over the countryside.'

'Quite right, sir,' agreed Lady Wyre. 'I hope you will tell her that everything is in hand and I shall come and see her myself as soon as I return, to tell her how things stand. She need not distress herself further over the matter.'

'Will you be coming with us, Hauxwell?'

Sir Thomas's question brought Miss Sedgewick's wandering attention firmly back to the breakfast-table.

'No. My spirits are in need of a little entertainment this morning. I have a mind to

116

join the others in the music-room. Will you come with me, Miss Sedgewick?'

She looked up, startled. 'I? Oh — no, no thank you.'

Mr Hauxwell rose and with a bow to the assembled company, he left the room.

'I thought I might seek out Mama,' said Madeleine, rising.

'She will be pleased to see you, I am sure,' said Sir Thomas, 'for she has this very morning received a letter from London, and I ordered it to be taken along to her room. 'Tis doubtless from your papa.'

'Then I must certainly go to her!'

'Yes, yes, run along, child and discover for us when your father means to return,' cried Sir Thomas in high good humour. 'I am sure we would all be pleased to see him.'

Without further delay, Madeleine departed. As she crossed the hall she could hear music and bursts of laughter coming from behind the closed doors to one side, but in her present mood she had no wish to join the merry-makers and she turned instead to a door on the opposite side of the hall that opened into the library, from which room a connecting door led into the west wing, where Sir Thomas's guests were accommodated in apartments linked by a narrow corridor. As this passage formed the only access to the rooms, Miss Sedgewick was in no way surprised to see a servant coming towards her. As he passed, she recognized Mr Hauxwell's man, tenderly bearing away a pair of his master's boots for polishing. She met no one else as she walked the length of the corridor and the only sound to disturb the silence was the whisper of her own skirts as she moved.

Suddenly it came to her, an idea so audacious that she stopped, wondering if she dare execute such a plan. She glanced back along the corridor: it was deserted. Before her were the blank, closed doors of the guest apartments. From one of these had come Mr Hauxwell's valet. She knew that her parents' room led from the two end doors, and next to them was the Comte du Vivière. From her childhood visits to the house she knew the room occupied by her cousin and its two adjoining apartments were smaller rooms, more suited to single gentlemen. It should be very easy to ascertain which room had been given to Mr Hauxwell.

Taking a deep breath, Madeleine moved to the nearest door and tapped gently. There was no reply. She had expected that, for the breakfast hour was well advanced and the servants had long since completed their tasks and departed. Slowly she turned the handle.

The door opened and she stepped into the room, silently closing the door behind her. To her right, was the dividing wall and door that separated this chamber from its dressing-room, which also doubled as a servant's bedroom. To her left a tall chest of drawers stood against the wall, leaving barely walking space between its bowed front and the side of the bed which was an old, heavily carved piece of furniture, the canopy and damask hangings of which looked out of place in such a small room. Now that she was in the chamber, Miss Sedgewick was at a loss to know what she was hoping to find. It was without doubt Mr Hauxwell's apartment, for his initials were boldly emblazoned upon a small travelling case which rested on the chest of drawers. Glancing around her, she saw a gentleman's greatcoat thrown over the back of a chair beside the window. She moved purposefully across the room and, hardly believing her own temerity she reached into one of the coat's capacious pockets. Her fingers touched cold metal and she carefully pulled out a deadly looking pistol.

A cold fear clutched at her stomach and for a brief moment Madeleine thought she might faint. It was not unusual for a gentleman to carry a weapon when travelling, but such things were generally holstered in the carriage, or the saddle, certainly not secreted in the pocket of a greatcoat. She knew a little about firearms, but she had never seen a holster pistol such as this: its slim, octagonal barrel, the fore and rear sights hinted at a much more specialized weapon, such as a duelling pistol. Suddenly her straining ears caught a slight sound from the corridor. Footsteps were approaching. She quickly thrust the pistol back into the pocket and turned towards the dressing-room, then she stopped. To reach the dressing-room door, she would have to cross the room and risk being seen by anyone entering. She turned back towards the heavy bed-hangings and hid herself in their voluminous folds. Scarcely daring to breathe, she heard the door open and someone enter the room. After that she heard nothing but the thud of her own heart. The heavy cloth enveloped her in its dark folds, pressing against her face and she fought against the desire to sneeze. She clenched her teeth and tried to remain motionless, praying that whoever had entered would leave again very soon. But even as she uttered up her silent prayer, the curtain was whisked aside and she found herself confronting the stern-faced Beau Hauxwell, the wickedly gleaming point of his unsheathed sword-stick at her throat.

8

The gentleman was the first to break the silence.

'My dear Miss Sedgewick — what an unexpected pleasure.' He returned the thin steel blade to its holder, and it became once more an innocent-looking silver-topped cane.

'I-I was on my way to Mama and mistook the door and — er — panicked.'

It sounded unconvincing, even to Madeleine, and she found herself flushing guiltily.

'Oh come now, in a house you have known all your life? I am sure you can do better than that,' he drawled, moving towards her.

Miss Sedgewick pressed herself back against the hangings and felt the solid wall behind her.

'Please, do not come any closer, or I shall scream!'

He looked amused, but retired a little and sat down upon the edge of the bed, still effectively blocking her escape.

'May I know the real reason for your visit?' he enquired. 'I am forced — regretfully — to conclude that your intentions are not of — ah — an amorous nature.' She blushed fierily.

'Or perhaps — how stupid of me! You expected to find your cousin. His room is next door to this.'

Her eyes flashed. 'You are insulting, sir!'

His brows rose. 'My dear girl, I return from my breakfast to find you hiding in my room, you give me no plausible explanation: surely you cannot blame me for a little conjecture.' His reasonable tone only fanned the flame of her anger, but at the same time she felt a childish desire to burst into tears.

'How dare you ridicule me! I will listen to no more of this. Let me leave at once.'

'Now I have offended you. Forgive me.' He caught her hand as she tried to pass him. 'You are trembling pitifully, child. What have I done to make you so afraid of me? Will you not tell me what has upset you?'

Madeleine drew her hand away, saying in a low voice, 'I have already explained my mistake. Please — I wish to go.'

The piercing blue eyes studied her face for a long moment, then he rose and walked to the foot of the bed, allowing her room to pass.

'Very well. If that is your wish.'

She hurried to the door, but as she reached it he spoke again.

'Miss Sedgewick! I would like you to know that I am not your enemy. If there is anything troubling you, you may safely confide in me.'

She could not look at him.

'Thank you,' she muttered, before hurrying out of the room in confusion.

★ ★ ★

Miss Sedgewick spent the next hour with her mama, sitting quietly while her father's letter was read aloud to her and entering into her mother's sentiments upon every point it contained. In reality, however, her mind was in turmoil. Anger, shame and fear warred within her. Bad enough that she had decided to enter a gentleman's room, but to be discovered there! Her greatest dilemma was what she should do now. The problem haunted her for the rest of the morning, and she felt in desperate need of a confidante, yet when she met her cousin later in the day she found herself strangely loath to unburden herself. As the dinner hour approached, Madeleine felt her situation was becoming intolerable. She had kept to her room for most of the day to avoid meeting Mr Hauxwell, but she knew she could not remain there indefinitely.

Oh I wish Papa was here to advise me, was her unspoken thought, but Miss Sedgewick was a sensible young lady and she did not long indulge in fruitless wishing. Instead she changed into her most sober evening dress of holly green velvet, bade Sarah dress her hair in simple curls then, hoping that she looked suitably serious, she left her room and went in search of Sir Thomas.

*   *   *

Having been informed that her host was in his study, Miss Sedgewick quickly made her way downstairs to Sir Thomas's ground-floor office, where the business of the estate was carried out. Entering the room, with its dark wood-panelled walls and sturdy, functional furniture, Madeleine stood irresolute at the door, uncertain how to begin. Sir Thomas was seated at his desk but he rose, smiling, when he saw her.

'Maddie, my dear! Has Lady Wyre sent you to drag me away from my ledgers?'

'Not quite,' she smiled perfunctorily. 'I came to ask your advice, sir.'

He spread his hands. 'Certainly, child. How may I help you?'

She looked down at her hands, folded tightly together.

'It — it concerns one of your guests — Mr Hauxwell. I think — I think he is involved in the murder of the Frenchman!' She finished her speech in a rush and paused, half-expecting him to laugh at her fears. Looking up, she found her host regarding her gravely.

'Do you, indeed? And what makes you think he is connected with such a thing?'

'I cannot prove anything, of course, but yesterday, it was mentioned that someone had been disturbed while prowling about the lodgings where the Frenchman was staying.' She fixed her anxious gaze upon Sir Thomas. 'I saw Mr Hauxwell coming out of the South Wood just after dawn yesterday. He was very muddy, as though he had been walking for some distance, say from the village.'

'You cannot be sure that is the case. Why, there is nothing unusual in a gentleman setting out for an early morning walk.'

'No, I am aware of that, sir. Yet later that same day, Mr Hauxwell excused himself from riding out with us because it was too dirty, but he *did* go out riding, alone, shortly after we had left. It does not make sense.'

Sir Thomas allowed himself a slight smile.

'I fear you are making too much of these circumstances,' he said gently. 'Many of my guests rise early, for a variety of reasons. It is possible that his sleep was disturbed by your father's departure, is it not?'

'Yes, of course, but the circumstance of his

being the one to find the body . . . '

He came up to her and placed his hands upon her shoulders.

'Madeleine, you are allowing your imagination too free a rein,' he interrupted her gently but firmly. 'This is mere conjecture.'

'But he has a pistol!' she declared in desperation.

'My dear girl, a good many gentlemen carry firearms.'

'But they do not usually keep them in their coat pockets when staying at Wyre Hall.'

For one fearful moment Madeleine thought he was going to ask her how she had come by such information, but to her relief he merely walked away to the fire, a slight frown creasing his brow.

'You are making too much of these things, Maddie,' he said at last. 'You must believe me when I tell you Hauxwell is no murderer. I think perhaps the tragic events of yesterday have overset your judgement in this matter.'

'Do you really believe that?' She looked at him hopefully.

'Yes, I do.' He smiled, 'Why, Hauxwell is a person of some standing in Town, related to some of the best families, and a friend of the Prince, too — not that *that* is any great recommendation,' he added drily. 'No, dash it, he's a true Englishman, Maddie, take my word for it.'

'Then I have wasted your time, sir.'

'Not at all, child. I am only too pleased that you have come to me with your suspicions and would beg that you continue to do so, if anything worries you. But I hope that for the moment I have set your mind at rest. Now, let us go upstairs before my lady sends a footman to look for us. It won't do to keep our guests waiting for their dinner, now will it? And tell me what news there is of your Papa,' he continued as they left the study. 'I trust his letter to your mother brought her good tidings?'

'Yes, indeed, Sir Thomas. Papa says he has already seen Lord Grenville, and the threat of immediate war seems to have receded. He believes now that the peace will hold until after Christmas. Papa writes that there is very little for him to do in Town in the meantime and he hopes to be with us again in a few days.'

'This is excellent news,' declared Sir Thomas, 'I am sure you will be delighted to have him safe with you again.'

'Yes. Mama especially feels his absence most acutely.'

They were approaching the drawing-room by this time and Sir Thomas stopped.

'To go back to that other little matter, Madeleine. Have you mentioned your suspicions to anyone else? No? Good, then if you will be guided by me, we will keep this little talk to ourselves. It is a very serious matter to lay such a charge at a gentleman's door.'

'Oh I know that,' came the earnest reply. 'I have been in torment all day trying to decide what is best to do.'

'You chose the right course in coming to me,' he assured her. 'I hope you will now be easy upon that head. St John Crossley, our local magistrate, is an old acquaintance of mine and you may rest assured that he will do everything in his power to bring the real villain to justice.'

★ ★ ★

Miss Sedgewick could not completely banish her suspicions, but having laid open her thoughts to Sir Thomas, she felt obliged to follow his advice and did her best to forget the matter. She dreaded meeting Mr Hauxwell at dinner, but when he entered the room the gentleman gave no indication by word or gesture that he recalled their earlier meeting, which greatly relieved Miss Sedgewick of one worry, although it served to heighten her regret at having acted so rashly.

After dinner, Madeleine fetched her tambour frame and made herself comfortable in a quiet corner, giving her attention to her embroidery. She was alarmed to see Mr Hauxwell approaching her and began hurriedly to fold up her work.

'Oh please, I beg you will not go,' he said, pulling up a chair. 'If you run away every time I come near you, how am I ever going to forgive myself for walking in upon you this morning in such an unfortunate manner?'

She glanced around anxiously but was relieved to see that there was no one near enough to hear his words.

'If it is your intention that my remorse over that sorry episode should be increased, you are succeeding only too well,' she told him in a low voice.

'But that is not at all what I want. Come, Miss Sedgewick, be done with this self-reproach. You told me this morning you had mistaken your way — very well, that is not impossible — and when you heard someone approach it is not at all surprising that you were panicked into secreting yourself behind the hangings of the bed. It is a very reasonable explanation.'

She eyed him suspiciously, but he met her look with such an open gaze that she relaxed slightly.

'If I have wronged you, sir, you may be sure I am truly sorry for it.'

He rose. 'My dear Miss Sedgewick, it is not my desire that you should be sorry for anything.' With this, and a graceful bow, he moved away.

Madeleine was so engrossed with her own worries that she paid little heed to anyone else that evening and it was with some surprise that she welcomed Cassandra to her chamber shortly after they had retired. Madeleine was sitting at her dressing-table, where Sarah was brushing out her soft brown curls. Perceiving Cassandra's troubled countenance, she dismissed her maid and smiled warmly at her friend.

'That is much better, we can be comfortable now that we are alone. What did you wish to talk about, Cassie?'

'Oh, nothing in particular,' came the reply, a trifle too casually. 'I could not sleep and I thought you might care for a little company.'

Observing the expressive little face from her mirror, Miss Sedgewick was not deceived by this apparent nonchalance, but she merely smiled.

'Certainly, but it must not be for too long, for your mama will be certain to lay the blame at my door if you are not in your best looks for the ball tomorrow.'

'Oh that.' Cassandra shrugged dismissively.

'Come now, Cassie, are you going to tell me you are not excited at the prospect? Why, your mama tells me you have a splendid new gown for the occasion. I hope Lord Kilmer will be suitably impressed.'

'I am sure I do not care what he thinks!' declared Miss Wyre, looking quite forlorn.

'Oh dear, have you quarrelled again?'

'Not exactly. In fact, it is quite the contrary: I am free to do and say what I please; Kilmer informs me it is not his place to criticize me.' She stopped, then burst out, 'I do not understand him, Maddie. He is everything that is most correct, but I feel he is doing his duty, as if to a stranger. He is so distant. I can perceive no sign of affection in him. In Town he was so desirous to please me yet here . . . Why, Mr Fulbeck pays me more compliments than Kilmer, and he frowns a good deal less. I begin to think it would be a mistake to accept any offer of Kilmer's — should he make one.'

'Perhaps it is your encouragement of Mr Fulbeck that sets his lordship at a distance.'

Cassandra looked obstinate.

'And why should I not be friendly with the gentleman? He is perfectly charming.'

'I know very little of Lord Kilmer,' said Madeleine carefully, 'but he does not appear

131

to be a very demonstrative gentleman. I think perhaps you are dazzled by the attentions of the other gentlemen here, and thus comparing his lordship unfavourably.'

'And would not you do the same?' retorted Cassandra defensively. 'The other gentlemen are all so entertaining — *they* do not find fault with my behaviour. I find his lordship quite tedious.'

'I do not believe you mean that, Cassie.'

Miss Wyre took out a handkerchief and dabbed at her eyes.

'I am not sure what I mean any more.'

'Well, Fulbeck is very charming,' observed Madeleine, pretending to consider the matter. 'He is full of rattling nonsense, and can be relied upon to enliven any gathering. However, if I were in need of help, or advice, it would be to his lordship that I would turn.'

'You would?' asked her friend, wide-eyed.

'But of course! These rattling types are usually quite empty headed, you know, and of no use whatever in a crisis. No, Kilmer is definitely the more practical gentleman, even though he does not wear his heart on his sleeve. I have no doubt that when you were in Town he was able to secure your comfort, procuring refreshment for you in a crowded supper room, for instance, or finding you a chair to take you home when there was an unexpected shower — a host of little actions.'

'I have never thought of it in that way,' said Miss Wyre slowly.

'One usually does not notice these things, only the lack of them,' came the prosaic reply.

'Well . . . perhaps if I am a little warmer towards Kilmer tomorrow, he may respond.'

'It would be as well to stop trying to make him jealous of Fulbeck.'

From Cassandra's reddened cheek Madeleine knew her supposition had been correct. She continued in a milder tone, 'Doubtless you would like Lord Kilmer to snatch you away and challenge his rival to a duel, or some such dangerous nonsense, but I fear you have mistaken your man, Cassie. If you push him too far, heaven knows what the consequences might be.'

'Of course I do not wish him to fight a duel for me,' was the unconvincing reply, which made Miss Sedgewick smile.

'No, that is an absurd notion, is it not? Now, off you go to bed, Cassie, and tomorrow put on your prettiest gown. Show his lordship what a very dignified and demure young lady you can be.'

Miss Wyre's vivacious countenance was lit by a sudden, mischievous smile.

'That would be so much out of character

that Mama would be sure to say I was sickening for something and call in Dr Tibbs!'

★   ★   ★

The following morning Miss Wyre did indeed look very fetching in a cream morning gown of soft wool with a snowy white neckerchief crossing at the bodice and tied in a large frothy bow behind her. She gave Madeleine a cheerful smile when they met, but there was no opportunity for private speech and the main topic of conversation at breakfast was the ball to be held that night.

'I do hope none of your guests has far to travel, Sir Thomas?' remarked Mrs Eldwick, 'It is such a shame if inclement weather prevents a full attendance.'

'Oh, I have very little fear of that, ma'am. The furthest has but ten miles to cover, which is nothing with a good moon to light the way.'

'And there is every chance it will be a clear night,' put in Mr Fulbeck, glancing out of the window.

'Is it true you have hired musicians from London to play for us, Papa?' asked Mrs Westlake.

'Aye, Jane. Some of the very finest.' He glanced around at the assembled company.

'So I shall expect everyone to join in the dancing!'

Mrs Westlake, who was sitting beside Madeleine, blushed and smiled, saying quietly, 'I know Papa does not include *me* in his plans. I shall be sorely tempted to take my place on the dance floor, I can tell you, for you know I have a veritable passion for dancing. However, I must not exert myself too much in my present *delicate* condition. Mr Westlake worries so for me, poor lamb.'

Observing the singularity of purpose with which the 'poor lamb' was addressing himself to a full plate of victuals, Miss Sedgewick found it difficult to pity him.

Later, they all drifted away to amuse themselves until dinnertime. Sir Thomas had organized a shooting party for those sporting gentleman who wanted to try their luck with the game in the South Wood, and the others whiled away their time at billiards or in the library, where their host's extensive selection of books and periodicals was at their disposal. Most of the ladies found their way to the morning-room, where they amused themselves with such gentle pursuits as embroidery or sketching. In the grand saloon, set between the dining-room and the drawing-room, a small army of servants was at work cleaning the chandeliers and mirrors in readiness for the evening's entertainment and an air of excitement permeated the house. The weather had improved to such an extent that Madeleine persuaded her mama to take a gentle stroll in the gardens. Overnight, the last of the rain clouds had disappeared, allowing the sun to shine unchecked upon Wyre Hall and its surroundings for the whole day and it held the promise of being a clear, if cold night, with a full moon to aid those travellers who intended to drive home after the ball.

By three o'clock, Sir Thomas's guests were all safely closeted in their rooms, preparing themselves for the evening's amusements. Miss Sedgewick could not suppress a tingle of excitement as Sarah helped her to dress. The gown was not a new acquisition to her wardrobe but it was a particular favourite. The figured satin bodice and close-fitting skirt accentuated her trim figure and the overdress of fine satin fell in soft folds to the floor and floated around her as she moved. The colour, a bold kingfisher blue, was both unusual and strikingly becoming. With a final touch to her hair, pearls clasped about her neck and hanging from her ears, Madeleine was ready to go downstairs. In the corridor she hesitated, then turned towards Cassandra's room, wondering if she should wait for her. However, she saw Mrs Westlake entering her sister's chamber and decided her presence would be superfluous. Instead, Madeleine carried on alone to the drawing-room.

★　★　★

Cassandra heard the tap upon the door and looked up from her dressing-table, but her face mirrored her disappointment when she saw her sister had entered.

'Oh, it is you, Jane. I thought it might be Maddie.'

'There is no need to sound so cross about it,' retorted Mrs Westlake. 'I have just seen Madeleine going downstairs, and wearing the most vivid blue gown imaginable.' She adjusted her own gold-coloured shawl of Norwich silk over her elbows, 'You would think, being so tall, that she would prefer something a little more . . . subdued.'

'No I would not think that,' replied Cassandra, firing up in defence of her friend. 'She is very pretty and attracts attention whatever she is wearing.'

'Well, you need not jump at me in such a horrid way; it was merely an observation,' replied Mrs Westlake, unperturbed. 'How you do take one up.'

'I am sorry, Jane, but Maddie Sedgewick has been very kind to me and I cannot bear to have anyone criticize her.' She eyed her sister resentfully. 'Why are you here, have you some message for me?'

'No, none at all. Mama is so busy with last-minute preparations for this evening that I told her I would come along and make sure you would not be shamefully late in appearing. Oh, what a beautiful fan!' Jane exclaimed, her eyes alighting on the open box on the dressing-table. She lifted the fan from its case and spread out the ivory sticks to reveal the exquisite carving, threaded through with ribbons of primrose satin, matching exactly the shade of Miss Wyre's ball-gown.

'Yes, it is very pretty. I shall probably carry it tonight.'

Jane peered at the card tucked under the edge of the box.

'From Lord Kilmer, is it not? Then of course you must use it.'

'I have not yet decided,' said Cassandra, irritated by her sister's superior tone. 'I have the fan that Mama gave me at my come-out. I have a mind to take that instead.'

'Oh come now, Cassie! You cannot seriously prefer that little painted trinket to this?' smiled Jane, laying the opened fan down on the dressing-table in front of her sister. 'I shall think you a most foolish child if you do.'

Miss Wyre had every intention of carrying Lord Kilmer's gift. Indeed she was secretly delighted with it, but her sister's smugness incensed her.

'I care not what you think of me,' she declared, getting up. 'I shall do as I wish.' She walked to the long mirror and studied her reflection, ignoring her sister.

Mrs Westlake's genius for uttering the wrong thing prompted her to say, 'Mama will be most put out if you do not make some effort to please his lordship. It would be most disappointing if all her hard work in that direction comes to nothing.'

Cassandra turned, her cheeks flushed, eyes over-bright.

'You are a hateful, interfering busybody, Jane, and I wish you would go away, before I quite lose my temper and throw something at you.'

'Well! You ungrateful wretch,' declared Mrs Westlake, shocked by this outburst. 'If that is all the thanks I get for trying to help, you may be sure I shall not trouble myself again on your behalf.'

She turned towards the door, but, as she swept past the dressing-table, the long fringe of her shawl became entangled around the top of a heavy glass scent bottle and brought it crashing down on the ivory fan.

For a brief moment there was silence, then, with a little cry, Cassandra ran forward.

'Oh now look what you have done!' she stared aghast at the fan. Three of the sticks had snapped and when she tried to gather it up, the broken pieces sagged heavily on their ribbon supports. 'Oh why did you not put it back in its box?'

'I am naturally very sorry for it,' said Jane, 'but if you had not been so ungracious, it might never have happened.'

Cassandra did not hear her. She sat down on her bed, staring at the broken fan.

'What will he think of me?' she whispered, 'What am I to do?'

'It will certainly do you no good to sit here crying,' said Mrs Westlake. 'You had best come downstairs and tell Lord Kilmer what has happened.'

'Oh no, I cannot do that!'

'Very well, tell Mama if that is what you prefer, but whatever you choose to do, you must descend to the drawing-room, and soon! There are at least a dozen extra guests arrived for dinner and it would look most odd if you are late.'

'You could say I was ill.'

Even as she suggested it, Cassie knew it would not answer, for such an announcement would bring Mama upstairs immediately and she would be compelled to put in an appearance, very much like a schoolgirl in disgrace. Even more than this, Cassandra's natural pride would not let her run away from unpleasantness. She stood up, resolutely drying her eyes.

'Mama will be wondering where we are,' she said, in as calm a voice as she could manage. 'We had best go downstairs at once.'

'Yes, of course. Only, let me straighten your sash first.'

Cassandra whisked herself out of reach, saying bitterly, 'Thank you, but I have had quite enough of your help for one day! If there is anything amiss, Mama can attend to it.'

Then she turned and swept out of the room, determined that no matter how disastrous the evening might prove, she would show the world a brave face.

9

Lady Wyre surveyed the assembled guests with quiet satisfaction: winter parties were always a risk, since the unpredictable weather could sometimes prevent the attendance of local acquaintances, leaving house guests to their own amusement. Thankfully, all those invited to the dinner had arrived and Lady Wyre was confident that she could expect a good attendance at the ball afterwards. There was no lack of lively conversation, and if Cassandra was a little subdued, Lady Wyre had no difficulty in ascribing the condition to a surfeit of excitement during the past few days. She was certainly not looking her best and her fond parent made a mental resolve to speak to her at the first opportunity.

After dinner, the guests returned to the drawing-room, where the wide double doors leading to the saloon had been opened, displaying this grand apartment in all its splendour. The floor had been cleared for the dancing and at one end of the room on a raised dais the musicians were already in position and tuning up in readiness for the evening's entertainment. Lady Wyre looked for her daughter and as soon as Cassandra entered the drawing-room she called her to one side.

'Cassie, my love, are you feeling quite well? I could not but notice that you were looking a little moped at dinner.'

'I am well enough, thank you, Mama,' came the quiet reply.

'Then do please try to look a little more cheerful,' begged my lady, 'I suppose you have worn yourself out with all your pleasuring. I am not surprised at it, for you will never take my advice and rest in the day, so it is no wonder if you are knocked up.'

'I am not at all tired, Mama, I assure you.'

Lady Wyre looked searchingly at her daughter.

'You are sure there is nothing amiss? Very well, love, then off you go and enjoy yourself, but you do not have a fan! I thought Kilmer would — he was certainly most anxious to know the exact colour of your gown. I — ' She broke off, glancing towards the door, a slight crease between her brows. 'Here is Lady Meeson arrived and no one to greet her — and Mr Greenley's party, too. Where *is* Sir Thomas? Love, I must go, but don't forget, you must *smile*!' She hurried off, distracted, leaving Cassandra to stare after her, feeling very miserable and forlorn.

If Miss Wyre's vivacious beauty was somewhat dimmed that night, by contrast Miss Sedgewick was looking her best. Her dress had drawn more than one curious glance, but she was unperturbed, for she knew the colour suited her and being tall she presented a very striking appearance. The Comte du Vivière had been placed beside Madeleine at dinner, which suited her very well, and he stayed in close attendance until the music struck up for the first dance, when he led her out on to the dance floor. As she took her place in the set, Madeleine looked about her for Cassandra and was relieved to see her standing up with Lord Kilmer. Assuming matters were proceeding well in that direction, Miss Sedgewick felt at liberty to relax and enjoy herself. She suffered a momentary embarrassment later, when Mr Hauxwell claimed his dance, but the gentleman's friendly manner and unexceptional remarks quickly set her at her ease. Soon after the dancing had commenced, he complimented her upon her skill.

'Thank you, sir. Your own performance is far from contemptible.'

'Dancing is a very necessary accomplishment for a gentleman of fashion.'

'Is that all you are, sir, a gentleman of fashion?' she asked him, a note of contempt creeping into her voice.

The gentleman looked pained.

'My dear Miss Sedgewick, I do not believe you can be aware of just how arduous a task it is, to maintain one's position in the polite world. For example, when I return to London in the spring, I have not the smallest doubt that my present coats will be out of style, and I shall be obliged to spend a tedious long time with my tailor, if I am not to appear behind the times, like some ridiculous country yokel.'

Miss Sedgewick could only be glad that the dance separated them at that point, for she had been about to utter some very sharp words. As it was, she curbed her temper, but when they came back together, she could not refrain from asking sweetly, 'Do you look upon us all as *ridiculous country yokels*, Mr Hauxwell?'

'Dear ma'am, of course not. How could you believe that I would be guilty of such impertinence? No, there are some here whose dress could not be described as being in the very highest kick of fashion, but it does not offend me, I assure you,' he ended kindly.

'I think, sir, that you are laughing at me,' she said suspiciously. 'I cannot believe you are serious about such a paltry subject.'

'Fashion — a paltry subject?' he repeated

in astonishment. 'I was never more serious, Miss Sedgewick. I have long studied the art, you know. Your own dress for example, is something quite out of the ordinary, yet you would not look out of place if you were to wear it to the most fashionable London soirées. The silk is Italian, is it not? The petticoat is hand painted and I would guess that you had it made up by a London modiste. Am I not right?'

She eyed him warily. 'Correct in every detail, sir, but while I am obliged to acknowledge your understanding of the matter, I cannot rid myself of the impression that you are deliberately provoking me.'

The disturbingly blue eyes held her own gaze.

'Now why should I do that?'

Despite her earlier reservations concerning the gentleman, Madeleine was enjoying herself.

'Perhaps because my eyes are at their best when I am angry?' she suggested, a dimple quivering at the corner of her mouth.

'No, no, I cannot allow that,' he replied gravely. 'I prefer your eyes when they are smiling at me, as they are doing now.'

She laughed. 'I think, sir, that you are a great deal practised in the art of dalliance.' she told him severely. 'Hush now, or I am likely to forget my steps, and just think how ill it would become *a man of fashion* like yourself to be treading on my toes!'

★ ★ ★

Watching the proceedings from the doorway, Lady Wyre was moved to comment upon her goddaughter's glowing looks to Mrs Sedgewick.

'I do not recall when I last saw her looking so well,' agreed that lady. 'I only wish Mr Sedgewick were here to see it.'

'She certainly appears to advantage with Mr Hauxwell. Positively radiant. Do you think it might possibly be a match?'

Mrs Sedgewick cast a startled glance towards her daughter, who was even now laughing at something her partner was saying.

'Oh dear me no!' she declared quickly. 'Why, she hardly knows the gentleman, and from one or two things she has said to me, I think she rather dislikes him.'

'I admit I know not quite what to make of him myself,' confessed my lady. 'To look at him one would conclude he is some Bond Street beau, with not a thought in his head but his appearance, yet when he can be persuaded to forget his affectations, he talks very much like a sensible man.'

'He has always been most polite and

charming to me,' agreed Mrs Sedgewick.

'I was a little afraid at first that he might turn Cassie's head, for she is very impressionable, you know, but if anything she seems to prefer young Mr Fulbeck.'

The note of unease did not go unnoticed.

'Kilmer has not made an offer?'

Lady Wyre sighed and shook her head.

'When we left Town I was sure it was as good as settled. I fear I have allowed Cassandra to be too complacent. She has blown hot and cold on the poor young man since we arrived here.'

'That is unfortunate. Perhaps she does not yet know her own mind.'

'Perhaps. Ah me, the joys of being a parent, my dear. However, Sir Thomas tells me I worry too much about these things, so I shall not say any more about it,' she replied, with a brave smile.

'I only wish we could get Madeleine comfortably settled,' remarked Mrs Sedgewick wistfully. 'After all, she is far past her majority, and not a hint of marriage.'

'Many girls reach two and twenty before they wed,' said her ladyship.

'Few that I know,' came the gloomy reply. 'And those that *did* wait ended by scrambling to catch any man they could!'

Lady Wyre laughed. 'I cannot see that

happening to Maddie!'

'No, perhaps not. In fact, I very much fear that she is developing a partiality for her cousin.'

'The *comte*? Well, he is a very charming young man.'

'But an *émigré*, my dear! He has nothing but his handsome face to recommend him and although he is a relation I cannot think it would be a good match for Madeleine.'

'It would not be ideal, I agree. Are you sure she does not like her partner? They look so well together and I am reliably informed that Hauxwell is *extremely* rich.'

Mrs Sedgewick sighed. 'I doubt if that fact would weigh with her, if she has set her mind against him. Madeleine very rarely changes her opinion once she has taken a person in dislike.'

In general, Miss Sedgewick would have agreed with her mama, but at that moment she was feeling more in charity with Mr Hauxwell than she had ever been; so much so that she allowed him to take her into supper. As they left the saloon, Madeleine noticed Camille approaching.

'Cousin, I was coming to look for you,' he said, 'with the intention of escorting you to supper.'

Mr Hauxwell bowed low.

'Ah, my dear *comte*, you have my condolences, you have missed your chance. Miss Sedgewick has granted that honour to me, don't you know.'

Madeleine was acutely aware of a tension between the gentlemen as they stared at one another.

'That is indeed my misfortune,' the *comte* said at last. He bowed to Madeleine. 'I shall come again later, Cousin, for you have promised to me another dance, is it not so?'

She gave him her warmest smile.

'Yes, and I look forward to it, Camille.'

'The *comte* is most attentive,' remarked Mr Hauxwell, as they moved on.

'He is a very agreeable gentleman.'

'Oh certainly. I am sure he can make himself most agreeable. Has he proposed to you yet?'

'Of course not,' she replied coldly, colour flooding her cheeks. 'In any event, it is not a matter I choose to discuss except with my closest family.'

He accepted the rebuff calmly and began to talk of something else, but Madeleine could not forget his words, and it clouded her enjoyment. She was quite content to be on good terms with her cousin, but she did not wish to think too closely about her feelings for that young man — at least not yet. Not even the sumptuous refreshments could restore her spirits. Lady Wyre was famous for her hospitality and her suppers were considered to be the best in the county, but Madeleine found she was in no mood to appreciate them. She responded to Mr Hauxwell's remarks mechanically and could not be induced to drop the cool reserve that set him at a distance. If that gentleman noticed the change he made no comment, merely continuing to keep up a flow of effortless small-talk until they had finished their supper. As he escorted her back to the ballroom, Mr Hauxwell cast a swift glance at the sober face of his companion and a brief smile lifted the corners of his mouth.

'You are a well-read young lady, Miss Sedgewick. Perhaps you might care to consider this: 'Ne let false whispers breeding hidden fears, Break gentle sleep with misconceivèd doubt.'' Her eyes flew to his face, a faint frown in her eyes. 'Spenser, and the message is sincere. I am your friend, if you will but trust me.'

'Oh but I was not — '

'And here is your mama waiting for you,' he continued, ignoring her interruption. 'Well, ma'am, I have returned your daughter safely to you. Miss Sedgewick, my profound thanks for the delight of your company at supper!' Then, with an elegant bow, he turned and sauntered away into the crowd.

Mrs Sedgewick shook her head as she regarded his retreating form.

'What a strange man!' she declared, fanning herself vigorously. 'I vow I am never sure whether he is laughing at me.'

'No, Mama,' returned Madeleine bitterly, 'he is not making May-game of *you*!'

Miss Sedgewick's naturally sunny spirits could never be dulled for long and that night she was determined to enjoy herself. She was in great demand after supper, dancing first with Mr Fulbeck and later in the evening Sir Thomas claimed a dance with his goddaughter. At one point she saw Cassandra going down the dance with Mr Fulbeck. Madeleine was aware of a slight pang of guilt that she had spared so little thought for Cassandra that evening. Another swift glance some time later showed her that Lord Kilmer was leading Miss Wyre out of the ballroom. Madeleine smiled and thought that she could safely return to her own enjoyment. However, if she had been privileged to hear her friend's conversation with Lord Kilmer, she would not have felt quite so complacent.

★ ★ ★

When Cassandra had entered the ballroom, leaving the despoiled fan on her dressing-table, she had been prepared for Lord Kilmer's questions. However, after one swift glance at her empty hands, that young man turned away from her to continue his conversation with Miss Eldwick. Cassandra was mortified, but her spirits would not allow her to show her unhappiness. Lord Kilmer claimed her hand for the first two dances, but made no mention of his gift. His demeanour was so rigidly correct that Cassandra had not the courage to tell him the truth. Instead she treated him to her most dazzling smile, but all her attempts to please seemed to that young gentleman no more than coquetry and at the end of the dance he left her without a word.

There was no shortage of partners for Miss Wyre and good breeding dictated that she should try at least to look as if she was enjoying herself, but never had Cassandra found it so hard to smile; even Mr Fulbeck's attempts to flirt with her met with little success when they danced together after supper. As Fulbeck led his partner from the dance floor, Lord Kilmer approached them. He was very pale and correct and at any other time Mr Fulbeck would have upbraided him as a jealous dog, but something in the young lord's demeanour discouraged ridicule and

Mr Fulbeck relinquished his partner with no more than a smile. Glancing up at her new partner's grim profile, Cassandra tried to jest.

'I declare you are looking most serious, my lord. Does the ball not please you?'

Lord Kilmer hesitated.

'Let us say that I am disappointed,' he said heavily. 'Will you not tell me, ma'am, if you received my gift?'

'Gift? Oh — the fan,' she said, with affected carelessness. 'Yes, I received it.'

'Well, madam?'

At this point it would have served Miss Wyre best to tell the truth, but she had been pampered and spoiled all her young life and had rarely suffered anyone's displeasure. She dreaded Lord Kilmer's anger and she did not doubt that if he knew of the beautiful fan, lying forlorn and broken in its case, he would be most dreadfully angry. It was too much to bear!

'Oh, well, I did not wish to carry anything this evening, sir. I wanted to remain uncluttered for the dancing.'

My lord's lips thinned into a tight, angry line. The movement of the dance prevented further immediate conversation, but as the music came to an end he took his partner's hand and led her towards the door.

'Pray, sir, where are you taking me?'

'Where we can talk in peace,' he ground out, still firmly clasping her hand.

'It may be that I do not wish to talk with you,' she retorted, two angry spots of colour on her cheeks.

Lord Kilmer stopped. They were outside the ballroom by now, at the top of the grand staircase, which was for the moment empty of guests or servants. He dropped her arm.

'No. I have come to the conclusion that you have no love for anything more serious than dancing or flirting!'

'That is not true! You know it is not true!'

'No?' He glared at her. 'I went to great lengths to procure a gift for you that would indicate to me your true sentiments. I made sure there could be no objection to your carrying my fan this evening. It was the perfect colour; your Mama approved it — but, no. You could not bring yourself to make such an open avowal to me.'

'My lord, it was not at all like that — ' She clutched his arm, but he brushed her off, too furious now for reason.

'I see how it is. You prefer to flirt with every gentleman here than to accept my attentions. Goodnight!'

'Kilmer! Where are you going?'

'To my rooms!' he flung at her over his shoulder. 'I will be leaving Wyre in the morning. There is nothing to keep me here any longer.'

Cassandra remained immobile, staring after him. From the ballroom the strains of a minuet flowed over her. She would not cry. Papa had taken pains to arrange this ball just for her, she must at least look as if she was enjoying herself. With something very like a sniff she put up her chin and walked slowly back into the ballroom, determined that no one should know how desolate she felt.

★ ★ ★

The night was well advanced when the *comte* eventually sought out Miss Sedgewick. She smiled as he approached, her eyes sparkling and cheeks flushed from exertion.

'Oh, Camille, would you object if we did not dance? I fear I shall drop if I do not have at least a short rest.'

'But of course, Cousin. I too would prefer not to dance,' he confessed.

She looked at him with quick concern. 'Is something amiss?'

'It is nothing — I have a little sadness.'

'How insensitive of me!' she cried, dismayed. 'I have been so busy enjoying myself that it did not occur to me that you might be missing your home. Let us find a quieter spot where we may be more comfortable.'

They left the ballroom and Madeleine allowed the *comte* to lead her to a small chamber off the inner hall. It was generally reserved for use by the ladies of the house as a sewing-room, but for that evening Sir Thomas had thrown open every apartment on the main floor for the convenience of his guests and they found a half dozen candles already burning in their sconces, and a cheerful fire blazing in the hearth.

'Peace at last!' declared Madeleine, sinking into a chair. 'I vow my head is ringing with music and chatter. I feel quite exhausted.'

The *comte* closed the door and walked towards her.

'You look enchanting, I assure you.'

She returned his smile. 'Thank you, Cousin. Will you not sit down and rest a little? I know Sir Thomas expects the festivities to continue for several hours yet.'

He pulled a chair closer to her own and sat down, staring thoughtfully into the fire. Madeleine watched him in silence for some moments, then she said gently, 'You must feel the loss of your family very much, Cousin.'

'I have a great desire to learn what is

happening in France, I confess.'

'Perhaps Papa will have news for you when he returns.'

'I hope so. To be so far away from everything one has ever known! I feel so *désolé*, so alone.'

Madeleine put out her hand.

'But, Camille, you are not alone, you have Mama and Papa, and myself. I know we cannot make up for what you have lost, but we are your family and I hope you will let us also be your friends.'

He took her fingers in his own firm grasp and raised them to his lips.

'Ah, Madeleine, without you my plight would be worse, oh . . . a thousand times!'

'If we can help you at all, in any way, you know we will!' she told him earnestly.

He turned in his chair, his dark eyes fixed on her face.

'There is one thing, but I should not speak of it. And yet — ah, Madeleine! You have been my comfort — my joy — since I arrived here. If it were not for you, I believe I would not care to carry on.'

'Camille, you must not say such things.'

'Must I not? But it is the truth, I know I have nothing to offer you at present, but that could change . . . '

Madeleine jumped up, her face very pale.

'Cousin, please, say no more!' She turned away and took a few agitated steps about the room.

'I have spoken too soon,' he said, following her. 'I know it, and yet I cannot help myself. When my uncle returns I will speak to him. Throw myself upon his mercy. Perhaps he will not think too badly of me for loving his daughter.'

She turned to find him standing very close to her.

'It will not do,' she declared unhappily.

He caught her hands and held them to his chest.

'Forgive me. I have imposed too much upon your generosity. I am but a penniless *émigré*; it was presumptuous of me to think you could feel more for me than pity.'

'Oh, Camille, it is not that.'

Madeleine stared helplessly at him, unable to find the words to explain her sentiments. She heard the door open and stepped back guiltily, pulling her hand free from the *comte*'s grasp. In the doorway stood Mr Hauxwell, surveying them through his quizzing glass. Under his scrutiny, Miss Sedgewick found herself blushing.

'Do I intrude? My apologies,' he said softly. 'Miss Sedgewick, I have been entrusted with an urgent message for you, from Miss Wyre.

She desired me to send you to her immediately.'

'Oh dear, I trust she is not ill?' asked Madeleine, her own situation temporarily forgotten.

'No, just a trifle overwrought, I believe. I came across the young lady a few moments ago. She was obviously distressed, but refused my offers to seek out Lady Wyre, or Mrs Westlake, and expressed a wish to see you, ma'am. She is even now gone to her room, and I told her I would find you.'

'Yes, of course, I must go to her.'

'Thank you.' Mr Hauxwell bowed, holding open the door for her.

With a final look at the *comte*, Madeleine left the room and Mr Hauxwell closed the door behind her. He looked at the *comte*, swinging his eyeglass idly to and fro on its ribbon between his long fingers.

'Your pardon, my dear *comte*. I trust I did not interrupt anything important?'

The Frenchman shrugged. 'Nothing that cannot wait, *m'sieur*.'

Mr Hauxwell smiled. 'You relieve my mind, sir. You cannot conceive how it would distress me to learn that I had impeded your progress with the young lady.'

'I had thought, sir, that you had an interest there yourself,' replied Camille, tight-lipped.

The gentleman laughed softly. 'At present, I have a much greater interest in *your* welfare, Monsieur le Comte.'

'There is no need to concern yourself with me, sir.'

'Oh, but it is my pleasure, sir!' returned Mr Hauxwell smoothly. 'I have developed a profound interest in you, my dear Comte. In fact, so great is my concern that I am quite desolated that you have none of your countrymen around you, and I have already set in motion certain — enquiries — to discover any acquaintances of Monsieur le Comte du Vivière who may be in England.'

'I would not wish you to go to such a deal of trouble on my account.'

'Oh, but it is no trouble,' came the smiling reply. 'I am looking forward to reuniting you with some of your old friends. In fact, I hope to be able to bring you face to face with one or two of them very shortly.'

'I am overwhelmed that you should show such generosity to a stranger, *m'sieur*.'

Mr Hauxwell made him a flourishing bow.

'Let us say, Monsieur le Comte, that I do it for France.'

'Then France will know how to reward you.'

Mr Hauxwell bowed.

'I hope sir, that we shall both receive our just rewards.'

* * *

Entering softly into Miss Wyre's room, Madeleine found her friend sitting on the edge of her bed, staring most dejectedly into space.

'Now, Cassie, what is this!' asked Miss Sedgewick in a rallying tone. 'I received a most disturbing report that you are troubled. Have you quarrelled with Lord Kilmer again?'

Cassandra looked up, her eyes bright with unshed tears.

'Oh worse, far, far worse,' she uttered. 'He is leaving Wyre in the morning.'

'What! Do you mean he is joining Lord Frederick's party?'

'No.' Miss Wyre's voice came muffled through the folds of her handkerchief. 'He is going back to Town. He — he says there is n-nothing to keep him here!' She dissolved into a flood of tears while Miss Sedgewick sat beside her on the bed, with her arms wrapped about her friend. At last the crying abated, save for the occasional shuddering sob that shook her tiny frame.

'Now tell me what has happened,' ordered Madeleine, still holding her. 'I had thought you were on better terms with his lordship.'

'He — he sent me a f-fan to carry tonight,'

162

sobbed Cassandra. Unable to continue, she pointed towards the dressing table where the box still lay with its despoiled contents. Madeleine walked over and took the ivory fan from its tissue-lined bed.

'It is broken!' she exclaimed, spreading the delicately carved sticks.

'It was an accident,' replied Cassandra, tremulously, 'but I did not have an opportunity to explain to Kilmer. He saw I was not carrying his present and at once drew his own conclusions.'

'As well he might,' murmured Miss Sedgewick drily.

'Oh Maddie, I am so unhappy! He was very polite to me at first this evening — he never even mentioned the fan.'

'And you did not care to introduce the subject.'

Miss Wyre shook her head miserably.

'I was afraid to do so, but later, when I had just finished dancing with Mr Fulbeck and we met Kilmer, he — he said he could see how it was with me and he saw no reason why he sh-sh-should remain at Wyre any longer.'

'His lordship sounds as if he is suffering from an acute attack of jealousy,' observed Madeleine shrewdly.

Cassandra shook her head.

'No, no, Maddie, you are wrong. He was

quite calm and — and rigidly correct. He thinks me a desperate fl-flirt and I have lost him.'

She dissolved into tears once more and Madeleine could do little to comfort her. A suggestion that Lady Wyre should be summoned brought an impassioned plea that she should not be told, Miss Wyre saying disjointedly that she had disappointed her mama and could not bear to face her now. At length she grew calmer and was persuaded to go to bed. With an assurance that she would come back before breakfast the next morning, Madeleine withdrew, leaving Miss Wyre's anxious maid to watch over her mistress.

★   ★   ★

By the time Madeleine entered the ballroom once more, the musicians were packing up and most of the guests had left. She discovered Mrs Sedgwick had already retired and, suddenly aware of her own fatigue, Madeleine decided to follow her example. As she left the saloon she heard her name and turned to find Camille coming up to her.

'How is Miss Wyre? Are you going back to her?'

'She is very tired. There has been a slight misunderstanding,' she replied vaguely. 'I have promised to see her again in the morning, but now I am going to get some sleep.'

He fell into step beside her.

'I do trust the young lady will be fully recovered by the morrow.'

'I have no doubt she will. Her nature is so sunny she can never be dejected for very long.'

He gave a perfunctory smile. 'Cousin,' he began, after a brief pause, 'has Mr Hauxwell spoken of me?'

'Nothing of moment,' she said, somewhat surprised, 'why do you ask?'

'I believe he wishes to set you against me.'

'Now why should he wish to do that?'

He shrugged. 'Perhaps he sees me as a rival for your affections, or perhaps — Cousin, perhaps he was sent here, by some enemy of France.'

She grew pale and glanced around the hall, as if to assure herself that they were alone.

'Do you mean, as an assassin?'

'It would certainly fit, following M. Breton's murder.'

'No, you cannot be serious!' she declared, horrified. 'I confess that at one time I doubted the gentleman, but Sir Thomas is well acquainted with him. He calls him a true Englishman and I do not believe my godfather could be so deceived.'

'Could he not?' the *comte* looked sceptical. He observed her troubled countenance and continued in a softer tone, 'But perhaps my situation makes me too sensitive. There is no proof, after all, but I would ask you to have a care in your dealings with this man. He could be very dangerous.'

They had moved to the foot of the stairs, where they stopped. Miss Sedgewick held out her hand.

'I do hope you are wrong, Cousin. I do not like to think so badly of any guest in my godfather's house. Goodnight, Camille, and take care.'

As she went to her room, Madeleine felt quite oppressed by the conflicting thoughts that crowded in upon her and she could only hope that a night's repose would bring some relief.

10

True to her word, Madeleine went directly to Miss Wyre's chamber the following morning and found her friend sitting up in bed, thoughtfully sipping at her hot chocolate. She greeted Madeleine with a bright smile.

'Oh I am feeling much better this morning!' she declared. Dismissing her maid with a wave of one dainty hand, she continued, 'I have made up my mind I shall confront Kilmer today, before he leaves.'

'Do you intend to throw yourself into his arms, Cassie?' enquired Madeleine, smiling.

Miss Wyre's dark eyes twinkled responsively.

'Not *quite* that. I was so sure of his regard for me when he first came to Wyre; I cannot believe he has suffered so complete a reversal of feeling. If I can but talk to him, explain to him something of my own sentiments, perhaps — perhaps he might be persuaded to remain. I know you will think me very forward,' she added defensively, 'but Kilmer and I have had no opportunity for private conversation since we left Town and I fear misunderstandings have arisen between us.

All I need do now is to put my case plainly to him and we can be comfortable again.'

'You make it sound very simple.'

'I hope it will be,' replied Cassandra, scrambling out of her bed. 'Ring for my maid, Maddie, and I will dress. I shall put on my new flowered muslin. I want to look my best today.'

'Shall I go on?'

'No, please stay, Madeleine. I would prefer it if we could go down to breakfast together.'

It was a full twenty minutes before Miss Wyre was satisfied with her appearance and the two ladies made their way to the breakfast-room. From the foot of the stairs they could see that the door was open and Lady Wyre stood on the threshold.

'Is Lord Kilmer not yet arisen, Mama?' asked Cassandra, glancing past her.

My lady looked at her in surprise.

'His lordship is gone, my love. I have just this minute taken my leave of him. I was most disappointed to have him leave so suddenly, and I want to talk to you later, Cassandra, to discover exactly what has occurred!'

'Gone!' cried Cassandra, growing pale. 'But it is scarce ten o'clock.'

'It is in fact half past the hour,' Lady Wyre corrected her, gently disapproving. 'He would not stop for breakfast but is returning to

Town and has said he will call upon us there in the new year. Now do come along in, my dears, for I cannot stand here longer. Lord Frederick and his party will be wishing to depart shortly, and I have barely spoken to any one of them yet this morning . . . '

She hurried away into the breakfast-room, but Cassandra drew back from the doorway, looking stricken.

'Oh Maddie, what am I to do now?'

'Go in and have something to eat,' was the practical reply. 'We may discuss it after.'

'How can you be so unfeeling? I could not eat a thing.'

At that moment a footman came out of the room, bearing a silver tray upon which rested a folded paper.

'Perhaps he has left a note for me,' said Cassandra, springing forward to take up the paper.

'I am sorry, Miss Cassandra,' said the servant, his wooden countenance betraying no sign that he had heard anything of Lord Kilmer's sudden departure. 'It is a letter for Mr Hauxwell. Sir Thomas is sending this one back to the hall since the gentleman has not yet left his room.'

Cassandra dropped the letter back on the tray and stepped back, disappointed.

'Oh how could he be so cruel!' she cried,

clenching her dainty hands into two tight fists. 'I must go to my room — I must think what to do.'

'But not before you have eaten something,' said Madeleine, firmly pushing her forward. 'We can decide what's to be done later, but it can only be to our disadvantage to have you fainting away from lack of food.'

The two young ladies took their places at the breakfast-table, where those guests due to leave for Lord Frederick's estates in Leicestershire were in high spirits. Their animated conversation so absorbed their hosts that Cassandra's pale looks and lack of appetite provoked no enquiry. Miss Sedgewick was relieved at the absence of both her cousin and Mr Hauxwell, for the animosity between the two gentlemen worried her and yet she did not wish to become embroiled in that dilemma until Cassandra's problems had been resolved. She persuaded her friend to take a cup of coffee, but a slice of bread and butter remained untouched on her plate and she appeared lost in thought. Madeleine finished her own simple repast then, in response to an eloquent look from Cassandra, she rose from the table and the two young ladies went out, their departure eliciting no more than a cursory nod from Lady Wyre as they passed her. As soon as they were out of the room, Cassandra stopped, glancing briefly around her to assure herself that they were not overheard.

'I have decided what to do: I must go after him.'

Madeleine stared. 'That is impossible, Cassie. You cannot chase the gentleman all the way to London.'

Miss Wyre shook her head impatiently.

'We can cut across country. With a carriage he will be obliged to take the main road to Guildford and from there go on to Leather-head, for all the other roads here are unsuitable for carriages at this time of the year. He is barely an hour ahead of us. We will soon come up with him.'

'We?' said Madeleine suspiciously.

'But of course!' replied Miss Wyre, opening her eyes very wide. 'Mama will not object if we ride out together and if *you* do not go with me, I shall be obliged to take my groom and he is *sure* to make a fuss when he learns my direction.'

'And with good cause,' retorted Miss Sedgewick. 'Forget this madness, Cassandra. You will be in Town again soon enough and can talk to his lordship then.'

'I did not think you would fail me, Maddie,' said Miss Wyre, searching for her handkerchief, 'My whole happiness depends upon your support. Besides, how do I know he will not offer for some other young lady if I wait until the spring to see him? Please say you will come with me.'

Confronted by a pair of pleading eyes staring up at her, Miss Sedgewick wavered.

'Oh, very well. I can see that if I do not agree, you will think up some other equally madcap scheme. At least it is a fine day for riding.'

She was rewarded with a brilliant smile.

'Oh I knew you were my true friend,' declared Cassandra, hugging her. 'Now we must hurry upstairs to change. I will send a message to the stables for our horses to be saddled up while we dress.'

'Very well, but I must see Mama before we go out and I will meet you in the hall when I have done so.'

Mrs Sedgewick was sitting before her glass putting the finishing touches to her toilet when Madeleine came in.

'My love, you cannot be going out already!' she exclaimed when she saw her daughter's olive-green riding habit. 'Why it was three o'clock when I went to bed, and although I could not find you, Lady Wyre was sure you had not retired.'

'I was with Cassandra, ma'am. She had

quarrelled with Lord Kilmer and was very distressed.'

'Ah yes. Mr Hauxwell told me something of that. I met him while I was searching for you last night. What a very strange gentleman he is, to be sure, for he began talking of goodness and sweetness being in you, or some such nonsense, which reminds me that I wish to talk to you.'

'About my goodness and sweetness, Mama?' asked Madeleine, a dimple peeping at the corner of her mouth.

'I pray you will be serious, if only for a moment,' replied Mrs Sedgewick, trying to look disapproving of such levity. 'I mean the gentleman's regard for you. I do hope you have not been raising false hopes, Madeleine.'

Her daughter looked incredulous.

'Most certainly not, Mama. I do not know what has given you such an idea, but I assure you I have offered the gentleman no encouragement at all. I cannot even say that I like him above half.'

'Well, that is what I thought,' returned her mama, relaxing slightly, 'but something Camille said to me last night made me think that he regards Mr Hauxwell as some sort of rival.'

'Well, he has no right to do so.'

'There is no need to snap my nose off, my

love,' said Mrs Sedgewick, surprised.

Madeleine flushed. 'I am sorry, Mama, but I fear it is my cousin who is indulging in false hopes.'

'But you cannot deny that you like him, and although it could not be called a good match, with the poor young man's affairs in such disarray while the present turmoil lasts on the Continent, if you are set on it, your papa and I would do our best to arrange matters.'

'But I am not set upon anything,' declared Madeleine, between laughter and exasperation. 'If Camille should approach you on the subject, Mama, I pray you will fob him off. I have no wish to wound him, but I could not agree to marry him, not yet.' She pulled a wry face. 'The sad truth is, Mama, that I do not know my own feelings! The more I try to consider the matter the more confused I become, for there is such a deal of sympathy in me for my poor cousin . . . ' She stopped, unable to explain the jumble of thoughts and emotions within her, and not even sure that she herself wanted to untangle them. With a bright smile, she said, 'Now, I am promised to ride out with Cassie and I must fly!' She planted a kiss upon her mother's powdered cheek and hurried to the door.

'Madeleine, take care, I have the strangest

feeling that you should not go.'

'Nonsense, Mama.' Madeleine laughed at the anxious face turned towards her, 'Cassie and I will be very careful, I promise you, but do not look for us much before dinner-time.'

★   ★   ★

Madeleine hurried away from her mother's apartments towards the entrance hall, feeling distinctly uneasy about the whole venture. She put little store by her mother's vague apprehension, but to be chasing across the country in pursuit of Cassandra's offended admirer was not at all to her taste. When she reached the hall, she saw the *comte* standing by a small side table. He had his back to her, but, as she approached, he caught her reflection in the large mirror on the wall in front of him and turned to her, smiling.

'Good morning, Madeleine. You are about very early, after so late a night.'

'Yesterday's good weather is still holding, you see, Cousin and the sun has tempted me to ride out with Miss Wyre.'

'Is it your intention to go far?'

'Oh, I doubt it,' she replied evasively. 'Most likely nothing more than a gentle ride around the park.'

The *comte* smiled at her, saying, 'The

sunshine very nearly persuades me to accompany you.'

'You would find it very boring, I am sure, sir.'

'Your company could never bore me, Madeleine.'

She flushed, but said archly, 'No, no, you must not flatter me, Cousin. Cassandra and I are going out to enjoy a *private* conversation and it would be very unchivalrous of you to upset our plans.'

'Very well.' He bowed to her. 'But perhaps I can persuade you to drive out with me one day soon, if the weather permits.'

'Certainly, and if you have no objection, I would very much like to take the reins: Sir Thomas helped to teach me to drive and I know he has sufficient faith in his pupil to allow me to handle one of his excellent teams.' She glanced around. 'Ah, here is Miss Wyre now, so I must take my leave of you, Camille.'

'As you will, Cousin. I wish you both a pleasant ride, ladies.' With a bow to the two friends he turned and walked away.

'I have ordered Amber and Snowdrop to be saddled up,' said Cassandra, leading the way. 'It will be easier to get away from the stable yard and I directed that the horses should be kept there. If they were brought to the house

I have no doubt that Mama would insist that we take our leave of Lord Frederick and the others before going off, and *that* would ruin our chances of success.'

'It is a little improper of us to be slipping off without a word of farewell, Cassie.'

'Oh stuff!' declared Miss Wyre, tossing her head. 'None of our remaining guests has bothered to come down to see them off — we are being no more improper than that.'

She led the way to the stables, which were built around a square cobbled yard and situated behind the east wing of the house. Entering through the high arched gateway, they crossed the yard, picking their way between the various carriages that were being prepared for the departure of Sir Thomas's guests.

'There's Snowdrop,' said Cassandra. 'I wonder why Amber is not yet brought out.'

As they approached the grey mare, a groom appeared at one of the doors, tugging his forelock as he informed Miss Wyre that her horse would be ready in a minute.

'We've been that busy, Miss Cassie, what with so many coaches to be put out and the like, that I left Amber to young Tom and the silly lad's put the wrong saddle on 'er. Jem is changing it now, miss. He'll be done in a cat's whisker.'

'You had best mount up, Maddie,' said Miss Wyre, imperfectly curbing her impatience, 'I will go and see what is happening to Amber.'

With the aid of a convenient mounting block, Madeleine was soon making herself comfortable upon the grey's broad back and she glanced idly round the yard while she waited for her companion. In one corner a gleaming black hunter was being led around by a diminutive stable lad, while a short, iron-haired groom looked on critically. She smiled when the horse took high-bred exception to a lowly gig that was being manhandled across the yard. He side-stepped playfully, snorting and throwing up his head. The stable lad was almost lifted off his feet as he clung on to the halter, attempting to hold the great animal. The groom stepped forward, taking the lead rein in his own hands and Miss Sedgewick heard him deliver a pithy lecture to the boy in a strong north-country accent. After a moment's hesitation, she turned her mount towards that corner and, as she approached, the black swung his big head round to observe her with a dark, dispassionate eye.

'A very beautiful creature,' she began, 'was he bred locally?'

The groom shook his head slowly, his

stone-grey eyes assessing her.

'Nay, miss. He's foreign bred — Limousin, in France.'

'Unlike yourself — I would hazard a guess that you come from the north.'

'Aye.'

'You are Mr Hauxwell's man — Stebson?'

'That is so, ma'am.'

'Have you been long with Mr Hauxwell, Stebson?'

He rubbed his chin reflectively.

'I've been with t'master, and his father 'fore him, while I were six year old.'

'Good grooms are in great demand, you know. Have you ever considered changing your employer?'

He shook his head emphatically.

'Nay, ma'am, and never like to do so.'

Miss Sedgewick's brows rose.

'You do not look like a man who would suffer fools gladly,' she remarked casually.

There was a glimmer of a smile in the weather-beaten countenance.

'Aye, miss. Thou hast the right of it. Ask any man who knows me!'

'Maddie, are you set? We must be off.'

Cassandra trotted over and in response to the urgent note in her friend's voice, Madeleine swung her mount away, leaving the groom to stare after her thoughtfully.

'We had best ride quietly until we are out of sight of the house,' suggested Miss Wyre when they were clear of the stables. 'Once we have left the park we can give them their heads.' She patted her mare's glossy neck, 'Amber is eager to stretch her legs — and Snowdrop too is very fast.'

'Then I trust I shall not be unseated and break my neck on this madcap errand.'

The comment brought a chuckle from Cassandra.

'You know very well you never come off, Maddie. You are a very good rider and we have hunted this ground together often enough in the past.'

'That was different.'

'Are you sorry you agreed to come with me?'

Madeleine relented. 'No, Cassie, of course not. I am just a little concerned about the propriety of this escapade.'

Miss Wyre giggled. 'Oh Maddie, no one could possibly object. After all, it is not as if I intended to elope or anything of that nature.'

Madeleine did not pursue the matter. Instead she asked, 'How soon do you expect to catch up with his lordship, if indeed we find him?'

'You need not worry about that. One of the stable hands told me he heard Lord Kilmer asking if the Guildford road was passable, or whether there was a shorter route to Leatherhead. Of course no one can be sure of getting a carriage through any of the other roads at this time of year, so we shall be sure to find him on the main highway.'

'I wish I could share your certainty.'

'You will soon see that I am right. We will head north and pick up the main road somewhere after Guildford. I learned at the stables that Kilmer is driving himself in his curricle with his travelling carriage following, so we shall have no difficulty in getting news of him.'

The bright sunshine was heartening and Madeleine found her unease diminishing as she settled into the ride. As they passed the park palings she glanced over her shoulder.

'We are well clear of the house now, Cassie. Shall we press on?'

'By all means!' declared Miss Wyre, urging her horse forward. The rain of the past weeks had left the ground soft, but Cassandra knew the country well and kept to the higher ground, well away from the marshy pastures. They took the western road across Hurtwood Common, preferring the hills to the gloomy wooded road through the glen a mile or so to the east. They slackened their pace as the road climbed steadily upwards and slowed to a walk, resting their horses when the land eventually levelled out.

'It is going well,' remarked Madeleine. 'We are making good time and the horses scarcely noticed the hill.'

'I do not want to press them,' replied her companion, 'it is a long downhill stretch to Shere, but after that we have the Downs to cross.'

A few more minutes of quiet walking and they quickened the pace again, leaving the common behind them as they rode down towards the village of Shere, on across the river and into Gomshall with scarcely a check.

'Do we carry on to Wotton?' asked Madeleine, coming alongside Cassandra. 'There is a track across the Downs to the Leatherhead road from there, if I remember correctly.'

'I think the lane off to the left, just ahead of us, leads directly on to the heath,' replied Cassandra, her eyes glowing with the excitement of the chase. 'Shall we try it?'

Her exhilaration was infectious.

'Of course.'

They turned their horses into the narrow lane between the cottages, passing a ragged urchin who stared after them open-mouthed. The lane rose sharply and soon petered out, leaving only a narrow track that led them up on to an exposed and windy heath. From their vantage point they could clearly see the Leatherhead road cutting through the landscape below them and a number of lanes leading to it from the Downs.

'Which route shall we take?' asked Madeleine.

'Any one,' returned her companion, 'provided we get off this breezy ridge.'

Madeleine laughed, enjoying the cold wind that tugged at her hat and made her cheeks tingle. She went ahead, cantering eastwards across the Downs until she was almost level with one of the lanes before descending to the farmland that covered the lower slopes. They soon found a gap in the hedge leading to a green lane and ten minutes later they emerged on to the hard surface of the highway.

'The first thing we must do is make enquiries, in case Kilmer has already passed this way,' said Miss Wyre with great decision. 'We have been riding for no more than an hour, I am sure, and he cannot be far behind.'

She set off along the road towards a cluster of buildings but there was no one in sight, doors and windows shut tight and even Cassandra disliked the idea of knocking on a stranger's door. Just as she was about to suggest they go on, Cassandra heard the unmistakable sound of hoofbeats and turned to see a rider coming towards them. His dress proclaimed he was a clergyman and without hesitating she rode over to him.

'Pardon me, sir, but have you seen a gentleman, in an open carriage — with perhaps a travelling carriage some way behind him? We are separated from our party and wish to be reunited with it as swiftly as possible.'

The parson frowned and shook his head.

'No, I cannot recall seeing any such thing. I have just now come from Ashtead and I passed no one save an old man with a few geese. Of course, it is possible that I passed your friends in Leatherhead and did not notice — '

'No, no, they would not have reached there yet,' put in Cassandra.

She looked helplessly at Madeleine, who said calmly, 'We have been riding across country and have somewhat lost our bearings — pray, sir, what is this village?'

'This is Great Bookham, miss. I am vicar here and if you should wish to stop and rest for a little, I would gladly offer you my hospitality . . . '

'No, that is, we are most grateful for your kindness, sir,' said Miss Wyre hurriedly, 'but we are most anxious to press on, before our friends become too concerned.'

'Of course, I quite understand.' He raised his hat to them and with a word of farewell went on his way, while the ladies turned their horses and trotted quickly past him and away along the road.

'We must be ahead of him,' said Madeleine. 'We will ride on to the next village and make further enquiry there.'

'Oh Maddie, perhaps I mistook, what if he is on some other road?'

'Pray do not lose heart now, Cassie. We made very good time getting this far and it is most likely that his lordship has been delayed. We shall doubtless meet him soon.'

Despite her cheerful words, Madeleine could not help feeling a little uneasy when they reached the next hamlet without passing anyone and an old man sitting in his doorway told them he had seen no coaches on the road that day. However, the ancient did suggest they might try the Bear, in West Horsley, as it was said to be very popular with travellers. Cassandra brightened immediately.

'Of course, I should have remembered it! I have often stopped there with Mama when we have travelled to Town. Come along, Maddie. Let us hurry.'

Rounding a sharp bend in the road, the

two friends came upon the hostelry set well back between sheltering trees, with a large courtyard to one side. They turned off the road and Madeleine heard Cassandra's sharp intake of breath when they rode into the yard and saw a large travelling carriage standing before them.

'Oh Maddie, do you think — ' She said no more for as they moved forward they perceived another, smaller vehicle and close by it a gentleman in conversation with the landlord. At the sound of the riders, the traveller glanced over his shoulder, then took a second and much more startled look.

'Miss Wyre!' he exclaimed, striding towards them. 'What in heaven's name are you doing here?'

Kicking free of her stirrup, Cassandra slid down into his waiting arms.

'Oh Kilmer, how glad I am to have found you. We have been searching for hours!'

11

Recollecting his surroundings, Lord Kilmer released Miss Wyre and stepped back a pace, flushing deeply.

'I beg your pardon. You should not be here — I cannot think it right — '

'I had to come!' declared Cassandra. 'How could you leave without even saying goodbye to me?'

'If I might make a suggestion?' interpolated Miss Sedgewick. 'Would it not be better if we all went inside? This is far too public a place for such a conversation.'

'Yes, yes, of course.' Lord Kilmer beckoned to the landlord and minutes later they were being shown into a small private parlour.

'This is much better,' approved Madeleine, stripping off her gloves. 'I am sure you can talk much more comfortably here.'

'You are not leaving us?' cried Lord Kilmer, as she went back to the door.

'Only for a short time, sir. Cassie says there has been little chance for you to talk privately, so I am giving you an opportunity to settle your differences, but I shall be happy to return with you to Wyre Hall, Cassie, if Lord

Kilmer wishes to proceed to Town.' She whisked herself out of the room, shutting the door firmly behind her.

She filled her time with a visit to the stables, where she assured herself that the horses were being properly attended, then she requested some hot water and the use of one of the inn's bedchambers in an attempt to tidy herself after her hard ride. She had no qualms about telling her host to add any charges to Lord Kilmer's tally, since she knew he could easily afford it and she reasoned that it was in any case partly his fault that she was at the inn. Returning to the parlour some thirty minutes later, Miss Sedgewick found Cassandra and Lord Kilmer sitting together on a wooden settle beside the fire, hands locked firmly together and such a look of happiness on his lordship's face that no words were required to tell her they were reconciled.

'Well, am I to wish you joy?'

Cassandra jumped up and ran to embrace her friend.

'Oh Maddie, we have agreed everything. Kilmer is going to come back with us today and will speak to Papa immediately. I am so happy.'

'Then so too am I.' Madeleine kissed Miss Wyre, then turned to Lord Kilmer, holding out her hand to him. 'I wish you every happiness, sir. I am sure Cassandra will make you an excellent wife.'

His lordship flushed.

'Thank you for your kindness, Miss Sedgewick. I am obliged to you too for accompanying Miss Wyre on this expedition.' He bowed over her hand. 'She told me you had doubts on the propriety of this venture. In any other circumstances, I would share them, but how can I disapprove of something that has brought me such happiness?' He turned to smile at Cassandra, who positively glowed with pleasure.

'I can scarce wait to see Papa. Pray, do let us return with all speed.'

Lord Kilmer shook his head.

'I have not yet eaten, and I had planned to breakfast here before going on. Perhaps, ladies, you would care to join me?'

'We would be delighted,' put in Madeleine. 'The ride has given me quite an appetite, and Cassie took so little at breakfast I wonder she has not yet collapsed with hunger.'

'I am not such a poor creature,' retorted a laughing Miss Wyre. 'However, I will admit to feeling hungry now, and would welcome a little food.'

A word to the landlord soon provided them with a simple but excellent meal of cold meats and pies and the three sat down at the table in the best of spirits.

'Do you intend to ride back to Wyre, Cassie?'

'Lord Kilmer has offered me a seat in his curricle.'

'You are very welcome to join us, Miss Sedgewick,' his lordship added hastily, 'there is room for three.'

'Thank you, but no,' replied Madeleine, her eyes twinkling. 'I have no wish to sit bodkin between the pair of you — I should be very much in the way! I have already decided to ride back the way we came. It is such a delightful day, I would enjoy the exercise.'

'But you cannot go off on your own, Maddie,' declared Cassandra, in shocked tones, 'If you *must* ride, you can follow us.'

Miss Sedgewick pulled a wry face. 'Follow a muddy road, and take twice as long about it? That sounds a very bad bargain.'

'But would it not be improper for Miss Wyre to travel alone with me?' put in Lord Kilmer doubtfully.

'Not in an open carriage, my lord. And I have no doubt your groom will be up behind you. I cannot see that she will come to any harm.'

'Well, if you are determined to ride back, you could take Amber,' offered Cassandra, 'she is the better horse for a long ride, and besides that, she hates to follow a carriage.'

Madeleine chuckled, but gratefully accepted the offer. They did not linger over their meal, but even so it was nearly two o'clock before they were ready to depart. Madeleine was soon making herself comfortable upon Cassandra's chestnut mare, who sidled and fretted beneath her, eager to be gone. But Miss Sedgewick waited until Cassandra was sitting in the curricle, with Lord Kilmer tenderly tucking a warm travelling rug around her knees.

'I will look for you at Wyre Hall,' she said, as the entourage moved off.

'Take care, Maddie.' Cassandra waved happily.

'Of course. I will not run your mare into the ground, Cassie, but even so I expect to be back at Wyre within the hour. I will tell them you are on your way.'

With a final wave, she turned Amber away from the curricle and trotted off along the road, turning into the first lane that would take her up and across the Downs.

* * *

Her mount took the hill at an easy canter and, reaching the top, Madeleine crossed the open country at a gallop, steadying the mare as they descended to the Guildford-Dorking road. She discovered she was several miles east of Gomshall, where they had crossed the road earlier that day, but she was making good time and not unduly worried about losing her way. Madeleine turned south-west and rode steadily towards the sun, skirting to the south of Abinger, and enjoying a gallop across the stretch of high open grass that led up to the dense woods of Hurtwood Common. The shadow of the trees now stretched out across the adjoining fields and as she rode into the shade, Madeleine checked her horse, aware of an indefinable sense of unease. Following her instinct, she decided against taking the lane through the trees and instead turned south, intending to skirt around the woods and take a more southerly route back to Wyre Hall. She went on at a leisurely pace, remaining in the shadow of the woods and had scarcely travelled half a mile when another rider appeared a short distance ahead, riding across her path. The horse was easily recognizable as the magnificent black belonging to Mr Hauxwell. The rider did not notice Madeleine, whose olive-green habit blended into the dark background of the trees. She hesitated, not knowing if she should hail the gentleman, or allow him to go on his way undisturbed. Before she had made a decision, a sharp retort rang out and the great stallion reared as his rider jerked back in the saddle. Without a second thought, Madeleine urged Amber forward and cantered up to Mr Hauxwell, who had recovered himself and was attempting to soothe his frightened mount. Madeleine noted with horror the dark stain spreading slowly across the left sleeve of his riding coat. He looked round, frowning as she approached.

'Miss Sedgewick! Go back — get away!'

Even as he spoke, another shot split the air. With a scream of pain the black reared again and sped away across the open ground, his rider trying to stem the head-long flight with his one good hand. Madeleine set her horse galloping after the runaway, unable to match the reckless pace, but determined to keep horse and rider in sight. A hedge loomed ahead of them: Mr Hauxwell made no attempt to turn the black, who jumped it easily. Madeleine had no idea of her mount's ability, but she could not imagine Cassandra owning a horse that did *not* jump, so she set the mare at the hedge and hung on grimly. Amber cleared it with nothing to spare and she allowed herself a faint smile of relief.

'Good girl,' she murmured, 'but how much further will he go, I wonder?'

The open ground gave way to a rough track through the woods but still the black plunged on, with Madeleine galloping behind. The mare was beginning to tire and she knew that they could not keep up the pace for much longer. Then, thankfully, the black's pace slackened: he slowed to a walk and eventually came to a halt, snorting loudly and trembling with fright. The rider was bowed over the steaming neck but as Madeleine drew closer he looked up, his face pale.

'You still here?' he said with the ghost of a smile. 'Why did you not ride home, silly girl!'

Ignoring this comment, she slipped down from her horse and went over to him.

'You are hurt; you must let me look at your arm before we go on.'

'It's Jove who came off worst,' remarked the gentleman, patting the horse's neck. 'The second shot nicked his ear. Poor old fellow, marked for life. But you'll do until I can get you back to Josiah. Josiah Stebson,' he explained for Miss Sedgewick's benefit. 'My groom. You met him earlier today — had quite a conversation, in fact.'

Madeleine nodded, but without a word she took the reins of both horses and walked over to a tree, where she tethered them securely.

'Let me help you dismount.'

'There is no need for that. It is merely a scratch.'

'You had best let me see it,' she commanded, as he dismounted stiffly. 'We must bind up your arm, for you cannot ride all over the country dripping blood.'

'How true. Very well, Miss Sedgewick, I am in your hands. Tell me, did you see my attacker?'

She shook her head. 'No, but he did not pursue us, I am sure. I checked several times while I was following you.'

'How very sensible you are. My dear girl, you are truly delightful.'

'I am not your 'dear girl'!' she retorted. 'Now, if you will help me to remove your coat, we will see just how badly you are hurt.'

'I am at your disposal, ma'am,' he said meekly, beginning to unbutton his coat with one hand.

'I am sorry if it hurts you,' she said, observing his sudden frown as she eased the coat over his shoulders, 'If you did not wear your coats so tight-fitting, it would be a great deal easier.'

'I will inform my tailor, ma'am. Perhaps there is some special style for people who are about to be shot.'

Madeleine chuckled, but made no reply. Gently she pulled the coat away from the injured arm, revealing the shirt sleeve torn and soaked in blood. She gasped.

'I am perfectly able to bind it up myself,' he told her, observing her white face.

'Nonsense,' came the bracing retort. 'I am quite aware that it looks the worse for all the blood around it. We had best remove the shirt sleeve.'

'There is a small pocket knife in my coat,' he said, sitting down upon a convenient tree stump. She found it quickly and lost no time in cutting away the tattered sleeve.

'You see I was right,' he observed, calmly regarding his arm. ' 'Tis but a flesh wound — bloody, but not dangerous.'

'True; you are much more likely to catch your death of cold from sitting around half-dressed on a chill December day. I will bind it up as quickly as I can. We have nothing with which to clean your arm — that must wait until we can get you to shelter.' She unfastened her white neckcloth as she spoke and began to wrap it tightly about the wound.

'My dear Miss Sedgewick, such sacrifice! Why did you not take mine?'

She shot him a sideways look.

'As a man of fashion, I did not think you would agree to such a violation.'

'After your callous treatment of my shirt, my dear, I did not think you would balk at

196

taking my cravat — ahh!'

'I am sorry, but I have to tie the knot tight, sir, to prevent further loss of blood.' she said sweetly.

'Witch!'

Madeleine smiled, but refused to be provoked.

'There. That is the best I can do for the moment. Should we try to put on your coat, do you think?'

He shook his head. 'It is soaked in blood, besides being too tight. I have a greatcoat strapped to the saddle. I will wear that.'

Without waiting for more, she ran over to his horse and soon came back shaking out the heavy grey surcoat.

'Let me help you. I think you should wear it on just one arm and we will button the coat over your injured arm. Are you well enough to ride?'

'Perfectly,' came the prompt reply. 'But will *you* be able to mount? I doubt I could lift you high enough with one hand.'

'That is no problem. If you will oblige me by holding the mare steady beside this tree stump, I will contrive to scramble up into the saddle.'

His blue eyes glinted. 'No doubt you would prefer me to avert my eyes?'

'Of course,' she retorted, 'but since I do not

intend to walk all the way to Wyre, I shall mount up even if you are unchivalrous enough to watch me. If it comes to that, I doubt if mine would be the first lady's ankle you had seen.'

'Very well, Miss Modesty, let us be moving.'

He stood up and after a rueful glance at the bloodstained riding coat, he emptied its pockets and rolled it into a ball before thrusting it into a small hole at the base of a nearby tree. Then he untied Amber and led her over to the improvised mounting block, dutifully looking the other way as Madeleine drew her voluminous skirts out of the way before putting the toe of her boot in the stirrup and springing nimbly on to the saddle. Within seconds she was securely seated upon the mare with her heavy velvet skirt falling in soft folds around her.

'What a very resourceful young lady you are, Miss Sedgewick,' he remarked, smiling up at her.

'Being a maypole is an advantage in this instance,' she replied, an answering gleam in her eyes.

'Are you considered tall?' he murmured. 'In my opinion you are perfectly proportioned.'

Madeleine bit her lip, not knowing whether

to laugh or be offended by his comment. She decided it would be best to ignore it altogether and she gave her attention instead to the darkening sky while her companion hoisted himself into the saddle.

'We will have to hurry if we are to reach Wyre before dark, sir.'

'We won't do it,' he said. 'The clouds will deny us what little moon or starlight there would be and I fear it would be foolish to attempt such a journey.'

'What do you suggest?'

'We cannot be too far from Dorking which was my destination today.' He nodded towards the east. 'The Horsham-Dorking road should be in that direction. If we reach it, then it is a straight route to the town.' He read the doubt in her face and added, 'Perhaps you would prefer to spend the night out of doors?'

'Of course I would not!'

'Then shall we proceed?'

They set off in an easterly direction and Miss Sedgewick glanced curiously at her companion.

'It is very late in the day for you to be travelling.'

'You will observe that I have an overnight bag with me, for I intended to stay the night in Dorking. More to the point, what were you doing so far from Wyre, and alone, too!'

She looked uncomfortable. 'Miss Wyre wanted to ride out this morning — '

'Chasing after Kilmer, were you? I heard the fellow had left in a hurry this morning. Lover's quarrel, was it?'

Madeleine was obliged to smile. 'Something of that nature. We managed to overtake him, and Cassandra persuaded him to return with her. I decided it would be preferable to ride home cross country.'

He grinned. 'No stomach for accompanying a pair of lovers, Miss Sedgewick?'

'They were gazing at each other in the most absurd fashion even before we set off.' She chuckled. 'What is it that makes perfectly sensible people behave like idiots when they fall in love?'

'I am sure I do not know, ma'am,' came the grave reply.

They rode on in silence, Madeleine glancing anxiously at her companion from time to time but apart from his pallor and the grim set of his mouth, he looked to be in no danger of falling out of the saddle. The light was failing, but before long they found themselves on open ground and could see a road stretching across their path about half a mile ahead of them.

'Unless we are sadly out of our way, that is

the Dorking road.'

'Thank heaven for that,' sighed Madeleine. 'With luck we shall find some village inn where we may put up for the night.'

'If you do not object, Miss Sedgewick, I would prefer to push on to the town. The light should hold for a while yet.'

'You are very anxious to reach Dorking, sir.'

He nodded, saying slowly, 'I suspect my attacker was trying to prevent me from meeting a certain Mr Jenkins, who should be waiting for me there.'

'Why should that be so important?'

'I had a letter from the gentleman this morning. Jenkins has some information for me concerning the Frenchman who was murdered recently, information that might help to identify the killer. It would appear someone does not want me to have that information.'

'You think the attempt upon your life is connected with M. Breton's murder? Are you . . . are you some sort of government agent?'

He laughed. 'No, no, let us say I am . . . an interested party. But there are certain similarities between today's attack and the murder.'

'M Breton was shot from behind, was he not? A most cowardly act!'

He looked at her sharply. 'How do you know that?'

Under his searching gaze she faltered.

'I-I think it was my cousin who told me. Why do you stare at me? Have I said something amiss?'

'No, I was merely surprised that you had been informed of such brutal details.'

'But what is *your* connection with the matter?' she pressed him.

'As I have told you, I am merely interested in the welfare of my country. I am hoping that the fellow I am to meet in Dorking will be able to give me some valuable information. If my suspicions are correct, then I shall explain a little more to you.'

'Are you from Bow Street?'

He laughed at that. 'Hardly!'

'You are not very forthcoming, Mr Hauxwell.'

'Later, I will explain everything, but until I have spoken to Jenkins it would not be right for me to say anything. I could be accusing an innocent man.'

'My cousin said you might be dangerous.' She watched him carefully, but he merely shrugged.

'Did he? Perhaps he is right.'

Madeleine shivered and glanced up at the lowering sky.

'I hope we reach Dorking soon. I have the distinct foreboding that it is going to rain.'

'Did you not bring a topcoat?'

'Of course not — I expected to be home hours ago.' She paused. 'I am sorry, I should not snap at you in that way.'

'It is understandable, Miss Sedgewick, in the circumstances.'

'Poor Mama, she will be so worried — ' She broke off, unable to trust her voice to continue.

The gentleman leaned across to cover her hand briefly with his.

'You will be back with her tomorrow, safe and sound, I promise you. Unless, of course, we have you laid up with influenza. Let us press on; I think we can reach the town before the rain begins.'

Twenty minutes later they were trotting along Dorking's High Street as the rain clouds obliterated the last of the sun.

'Jenkins should be at the Lion,' remarked Mr Hauxwell, leading the way towards a busy inn and, even as they approached, the landlord came running out to attend them. Mr Hauxwell's enquiries were met with a look of bewilderment.

'The gentleman went off to meet you, sir, about a half-hour since,' said the landlord, scratching his head.

'Oh? How can that be, since he knew not which road I would be taking?'

'One of the village lads brought him a note, and then the gentleman asked for directions to Wescott Wood, saying the fellow he was going to meet was being over-cautious, and had arranged another rendezvous.'

Mr Hauxwell looked grim.

'I'd best go after him. Westcott is on the Wotton road, is it not?'

'But your arm,' put in Madeleine, 'it needs attention — '

'Later. You can wait for me here.'

'Oh no!' declared Miss Sedgewick, gathering up the reins. 'I cannot understand any of this, but you are not going to abandon me at some inn and ride off into the night. I am coming with you!'

'I suppose it would be useless to tell you that you could be in some danger,' he said, trotting back out of the yard.

'Completely,' she agreed. 'Besides, I was used to hunt this area with Sir Thomas and I can show you the way.'

'Hurry then. It is growing dark already.'

'The wood is less than half a mile from here,' she said, as they reached the edge of the town. 'Do you feel well enough to canter?'

In reply, the gentleman touched his horse with his heels and the black set off at a fast pace, which left Madeleine's mare struggling to catch up. A grey dusk had settled over the land as they approached the small wood and Mr Hauxwell drew up, peering into the shady undergrowth. A narrow path led into the trees and he turned his horse towards it.

'We will have to go in,' he said, drawing a horse pistol from its holster. 'Stay close to me.'

Madeleine needed little persuasion to bring her mare nearer to the black. Once inside the wood she became aware of the stillness, and an eerie silence, broken only by the crackle of dead leaves beneath their horses' hoofs. Suddenly the great stallion stopped and Mr Hauxwell dismounted. Madeleine watched as he walked over to a mound of leaves a few feet from the path. He scooped away some of the pile to expose a white, lifeless face. In the darkness Miss Sedgewick could only see a white blur, but it was enough. She looked away, fighting the cold fear rising within her.

At last her companion returned to his horse.

'Is — is it the man you were to meet?' she asked quietly.

'I cannot say, but he has not been dead long. It would be a strange coincidence to have two men in this wood tonight.'

'How — I mean — ?'

'He was shot.'

'What do we do now?'

'Return to the Lion and inform the magistrate. If it is Jenkins then the landlord there should be able to identify him. Are you feeling unwell, Miss Sedgewick? I warned you not to come. I hope you do not intend to faint on me.'

His bracing tone had the desired effect.

'I never faint,' she retorted, hoping he could not see how much she was shaking. Carefully she turned her mare and preceded Mr Hauxwell back along the path and out on to the road, resisting the temptation to whip Amber to a gallop to escape from the terror she felt around her. They travelled back to Dorking in silence. Madeleine stole a glance her companion and was alarmed to see how pale he was, sitting stiffly in the saddle, his left arm hanging loosely at his side.

* * *

By the time they reached the Lion again it was completely dark, and a steady drizzle had set in. They rode into the welcoming light of the yard and without waiting for assistance Madeleine jumped down and ran across to Mr Hauxwell, who was dismounting stiffly.

'Quickly,' she called to the landlord, who

had appeared at the inn door, 'this gentleman has been injured and must be attended to. Do you have a private room we may use?'

Their host stopped and blinked at her. 'But of course, ma'am. This way, if you please. Ben, look to the horses.'

'You missed your calling,' murmured Mr Hauxwell, as they followed their host inside. 'From your excellent performance one would be forgiven for thinking I was at death's door.'

'It was the rain,' she replied. 'I have no wish to be soaked through while you explain the situation.'

They were shown into a small but comfortable private parlour which boasted a small table with a branched candlestick set upon it, several chairs and a smoky fire that the landlord kicked to life, sending a shower of sparks into the room.

'I'll send in the missus. She'll make you comfortable and if necessary we can send for Dr Potter. What's the trouble sir?'

'We were attacked earlier today.'

'He took a bullet in his arm,' added Miss Sedgewick, as she helped him to a chair. 'I bound it up as best I could, but the wound needs to be cleaned.'

The landlord gave her a reassuring smile.

'Now don't you fret, ma'am. The wife — Mrs Cubbs, that is — she knows what she's about. We'll soon have the gentleman feeling more the thing.'

Mr Hauxwell looked up. 'By the by, I think perhaps one of your boys should inform the local magistrate that there is a body in Westcott Wood. I would wager that it is your former customer, Mr Jenkins.'

The landlord's cheery face paled and his jaw dropped.

'Oh don't worry. I did not kill him. I think he was murdered by the same person who tried to kill me this afternoon.'

'Lord bless us, what's to be done!' cried Cubbs, throwing up his hands.

'Well, you can send someone to recover the body, and inform the magistrate that I will be pleased to see him in the morning. But for now perhaps you could arrange for some refreshment for myself and the lady — including a bottle of your best cognac.'

The good man withdrew, bewildered, and Madeleine turned to her companion. He looked pale, but completely in control of himself. He had retrieved his snuffbox from the pocket of his greatcoat and had opened it with practised ease using only his right hand. He regarded Miss Sedgewick speculatively.

'Is anything amiss, sir?'

'I thought perhaps you might oblige me by giving me your hand.'

'So that you may take your snuff from my wrist?' she laughed. 'No, I thank you!'

'But it will look so inelegant if I must use just one hand!'

Her eyes twinkled. 'I have heard that some gentlemen use tiny silver shovels for their snuff.'

He looked pained. 'Really, madam, do you imagine that I would stoop to such vulgarity?'

'No, perhaps not, but hush now, sir, here is our landlady to tend your wound. She would think our levity most unseemly.'

Mrs Cubbs came in, carrying a bowl of hot water.

'Good evening sir, madam. Mr Cubbs tells me you've been hurt, sir. Shall we take off that coat of yours and see what's the damage?'

With a faint sigh he put away his snuffbox and allowed Miss Sedgewick to assist him with his coat. In a moment both the greatcoat and his flowered waistcoat had been removed, revealing the spoiled lawn shirt, one sleeve already cut away, and in the light from the candles the makeshift bandage gleamed wet and crimson.

'It . . . it has begun to bleed again,' said Madeleine unsteadily. She dashed a hand across her eyes: the events of the day were beginning to take their toll of her over-stretched nerves, but she bit hard on her lip, determined not to weaken.

'Now don't you fret yourself, ma'am,' said the landlady cheerfully, 'I've dealt with injuries a dozen times worse than this. The gentleman will be up and about as good as new before you know it. If you like, you may sit yourself over there by the fire until I'm done.'

'No, I would like to help,' said Madeleine, peeling off her riding jacket.

Mrs Cubbs beamed at her. 'Very well, ma'am. I'll just go and fetch some clean linen for bandages, and we'll get started.'

While she was gone, Madeleine folded back the lacy cuffs of her shirt. Mr Hauxwell sat patiently at the table and submitted himself to their administrations without a word of complaint. The wound was soon laid bare and when the arm had been cleaned, Mrs Cubbs gave a sigh of relief.

'A bullet was it, sir? It's passed clean through the flesh, you see. I'll cover it with this before I bind it up and it should heal in no time.'

'What is it?' he asked, eyeing the small pot of grey ointment suspiciously.

'Why, it is only woundherb, sir. We use it all the time for cuts and swellings. I promise you it will do you no harm. There, that didn't hurt, did it?' she asked in a very motherly way that drew a smile from Madeleine. 'Now I'll bind it up for you and it should heal itself nicely. If you would like me to summon Dr Potter, sir, I'll gladly do so, but I see no need for it.'

'No more do I, Mrs Cubbs,' replied the gentleman. 'I've no reason to think it would heal any faster for having a doctor to look at it.'

Miss Sedgewick watched admiringly as the good woman deftly bound the strips of linen around the arm, expertly securing the bandage and tucking in the ends neatly to complete her handiwork.

'There,' she said at last, 'I think that will hold. It would be best if you keep that arm as still as possible, sir, for we don't want the bleeding to start again. I'll make you a sling, sir.' She handed a pair of scissors to Madeleine. 'You may as well cut off the rest of the shirt, ma'am. It is far past repair now.' She chuckled. 'Bless you, madam, there's no need to colour up so, to be undressing your husband in front o' me — you may be sure that I've seen a man's chest before now!' She bustled out of the room, still chuckling, and Mr Hauxwell's eyes positively danced.

'Come along, *Mrs Hauxwell*!'

'I shall explain the situation as soon as she returns.'

He grinned. 'I look forward to hearing that!'

'Oh do be quiet!' snapped Madeleine. She began tugging at the knot of his cravat, until Mr Hauxwell was moved to protest.

'My dear girl, you will choke the life out of me if you carry on like that! It is quite simple — you see, I can manage perfectly well with just one hand.'

He drew off the neckcloth and handed it to Madeleine, smiling at her in a way that made her long to hit him.

'One day I'll make you suffer for this,' she muttered savagely.

She found some small satisfaction in scoring the scissors through the fine linen of his very expensive shirt, and in a matter of seconds she was able to pull away the tatters without causing the gentleman to move his injured arm. She turned to throw the ruined shirt upon the pile of blood-stained cloth already on the floor.

'Well,' she smiled, as she turned back to her companion, 'that was easily done . . . ' The words trailed off and the smile froze upon her lips as her eyes alighted on a recently healed scar that stretched across the collar bone: a mark she clearly remembered seeing once before, on a grey and windy day at Rye harbour.

12

For a moment Madeleine's senses reeled and she backed away, unable to tear her eyes from the scar.

'Where — how did you get that?' she whispered at last.

He smiled. 'In t'service of my country, lady,' he said, his voice suddenly deeper and the northern accent very pronounced.

Madeleine sank on to a chair.

'I-I don't understand,' she said at last, frowning. 'Was it — were *you* the man at Rye who drove off my attackers?'

'The very same. Today's little incident evens the score, does it not? Though of course I shall not embarrass you by offering a monetary reward for your intervention.'

She put her hand to her head.

'Did I insult you with my guineas? I'm sorry. It was never my intention — '

'No, no, Miss Sedgewick, I was not insulted, I was enchanted.'

'But I do not understand.'

His smile broadened, but not unkindly. 'I will explain later,' he murmured, as the door opened and Mrs Cubbs entered, closely followed by her spouse, bearing a tray laden with dishes.

'I have brought one of Mr Cubbs's shirts for you, since I didn't know what you might have in your bag. If you will put it on, sir, I will then fix you a sling for that arm.' Her eyes fell on Madeleine, and she exclaimed, 'Bless you, dearie, are you ill? You are as white as a sheet!'

'No, no, I am well, thank you,' came the faint reply.

'Lord love you, child, we have been so busy patching up your husband that we had all but forgotten you. Now you just sit there and I will fetch you a nice glass of warm milk.'

'I think brandy might be more effective,' remarked Mr Hauxwell.

Madeleine glared at him. 'Milk would be very welcome, thank you.'

'Mistress Cubbs, I fear you may be under a slight misapprehension,' put in Mr Hauxwell. 'This young lady is not my wife — ' The landlord and his good lady exchanged surprised looks and he continued in a voice that brooked no argument, 'I would like you to have a room prepared for Miss Sedgewick, and have a bed made up in it for one of your maids. This young woman has been forced into a most awkward situation through no fault of her own — or mine, either, I might

214

add — but I am naturally concerned for her good name, and will have no breath of scandal attached to her sojourn here.'

Awed by this speech, delivered in Mr Hauxwell's most haughty manner, Mrs Cubbs bobbed a curtsy to Madeleine.

'I am very sorry for the mistake, miss. I meant no harm, I'm sure. I will arrange a room for you this very minute.'

Having set out the food on the table, the landlord followed his wife to the door.

'I've sent one of me lads over to the squire's house,' he said, 'but I doubt we will hear anything before morning. It's as black as pitch outside now, and raining, too. Now, I've brought you a good assortment of meats, and I'd recommend the game pie to you, sir. I had some for my dinner, and very good it is too. And I've fetched up my best brandy, sir, as you ordered.'

'Mr Cubbs, would it be possible to get a message to Wyre Hall? My family will be concerned.'

'Wyre Hall, is it, miss? West of Cranley? Well, no, miss, I fear the rain has set in for the night, and it's so black out there I wouldn't wager on anyone finding their way more than a mile from here.' He saw the disappointment on her face and added, 'I'll have breakfast waiting for you at first light, miss, and with an early start I daresay you can be home again before noon.'

Madeleine stifled a sigh.

'Yes. I am sure you are right. Thank you.'

Mrs Cubbs reappeared.

'Here's your milk, miss, and if you are requiring anything more, just call me. I shall be along later, to show you to your room.'

With a final cheery smile the landlady and her spouse withdrew, leaving their guests to enjoy their supper.

Mr Hauxwell drew out a chair for Madeleine at the table.

'A little food is just the thing for you, my dear. It will revive your spirits. I vow it quite oversets me to see you sitting there so meekly. You are in general such a *managing* female.'

'It must be a novel experience for you, sir, to be bullied by a woman.'

'It is, my dear, but I confess I am growing to like it.'

Feeling a blush steal into her cheeks, Madeleine turned her attention to the dishes set out before her. Since her companion was under strict orders from Mrs Cubbs to keep his injured arm in its sling and not to move it, Miss Sedgewick obligingly filled his plate with slices of ham and salt pork, followed by a generous helping of game pie.

'Now we are alone I would be glad if you

would explain everything to me,' she remarked as she filled her own plate.

He looked across the table at her.

'What would you like me to tell you, Miss Sedgewick?'

She met his glance squarely.

'You can begin by telling me why you were at Rye masquerading as a sailor, and how it is that you are now staying at Wyre Hall, and apparently a good friend of Sir Thomas.'

'Would you believe me if I said it was an elaborate plan to become better acquainted with you?'

'No, I would not. Besides, Cassie told me you were paying her the most marked attentions in Town.'

'Do I detect a note of jealousy there?'

'Certainly not. And it does not explain why you were dressed in common rags at Rye.'

He sighed. 'Very well, since you are determined to know the truth. I had just returned from France, and rich English gentleman are none too popular there just now.'

'Are you a spy?' she asked him, her eyes very wide.

'Not quite that, my dear.'

'Then what *are* you?' she cried in exasperation.

'Merely a gentleman who loves his country.'

'And which country would that be?' Madeleine

was startled at her own temerity, but he only smiled at her.

'England of course, you goose!' He pushed his plate towards her. 'Since I am forbidden from using one hand, perhaps you would cut up my meat for me.'

'Yes, of course.' She asked, without looking up, 'Did — did you kill the Frenchman?'

'Is that what the *comte* told you?' Her eyes flew to his face and he nodded grimly. 'I thought as much. Did he also send you to search my room?'

'No, that was my own idea,' she replied, blushing deeply. 'I discovered you had a pistol in the pocket of your great-coat — '

He reached across the table and gripped her wrist.

'Madeleine — look at me! Do *you* believe I am a murderer?'

Her gaze faltered beneath his penetrating blue eyes.

'I . . . no. I cannot believe it, and yet you *are* involved in some way. I wish you would tell me what you were doing at Rye.'

'I have already done so. I had just returned to England.'

'In disguise. You *are* a spy — it cannot be otherwise.'

'No, nothing so dramatic,' he told her soothingly. 'I was merely keeping an eye upon someone, and I did not wish the fellow to spot me. Tall Englishmen are rather notice-able across the Channel, you know.'

'So you disguised yourself.'

'Yes. I coloured my hair, changed my voice — long years of association with Stebson my groom came in useful there. Unfortunately the disguise proved too effective: when we docked, some fellow needed a porter and would not be gain-said. He paid me to carry his trunk off the quay for him and I was returning to the packet when I came across a couple of drunken sailors annoying an enchanting young lady.'

She summoned a shy smile.

'Then my heartfelt thanks to the gentleman who mistook you for a porter.'

There was an answering gleam in his eyes as he replied, 'Mine, also.'

Madeleine was already wrestling with the next question.

'If you were following a passenger on the packet, what happened when you reached Rye? Was that the end of your interest?'

'No. I continued to follow him. The man in question is a dangerous villain, but at present I cannot prove he is guilty of murder, and while he is free, our whole nation could be imperilled. Unless I can prove his guilt, it is quite likely that he will gain access to the

219

highest government circles, and there is no knowing what havoc he might create.'

Madeleine was very white.

'Camille arrived on the packet.' she whispered.

'I know.'

'It cannot be!' she cried, horrified. 'It is ridiculous. The Comte du Vivière is a solid supporter of his king! Why, everything he owned has been confiscated by the state — surely you do not think he could be in league with the very people who impoverished him?'

'No, I do not.'

'But you have just said — ' she broke off, the angry flush fading from her cheek as suddenly as it had come and she could only whisper faintly, 'What are you implying?'

'I fear the Comte du Vivière is still in France — in prison, mayhap, under a false name — and the fellow you call Camille is Danton's young disciple, Eugène Menotte.'

'Camille's cousin.'

'Exactly. He also happens to be a lawyer, which would explain why M. Breton was killed. He too practised law in Paris and would doubtless be acquainted with Menotte.'

Madeleine pushed her plate aside and stood up.

'No!' she cried, taking a hasty turn about

the room. 'I will not believe it. I refused to listen to Camille's suspicions about you — I will not let you tell me such things. They cannot be true. Why, he must be my cousin. How would a stranger know so much about my family?'

'Might not the *comte* discuss such things with his cousin?'

She sat down again, fighting back her tears. She remembered Camille's surprise at hearing of her uncle Robert's death, and occasionally, he did not respond immediately to his name, but these incidents were easily explained, she told herself firmly. They were certainly not sufficient to convict a man of murder.

'What evidence do you have against him?'

'Nothing conclusive. The morning I met you in the park I had heard the *comte* leaving his room very early, and I followed him. When he reached the village he made for the Bretons' lodgings. At the time I did not know whether Breton was an accomplice, and the dogs in the yard set up such a noise that he hurried away and I followed him back through the woods to Wyre. I have since learned that he discovered Breton's exact direction from Mrs Westlake.'

'But why did I not see him in the park? If what you say is true, he too would have been obliged to cross the park to return to the house.'

'I knew he would be returning to his room, and waited in the woods for nearly half an hour to allow him to get clear. When you met me I have no doubt the *comte* was already back in his apartment.'

'But there is no proof that he killed M. Breton,' she argued.

'No, I am sorry to say the *comte* slipped out of the house unobserved and it was only when Stebson brought me word that one of the stable lads had saddled up a horse for the Frenchman that I realized he had gone. He was a good half-hour ahead of me and it took some time to pick up his trail. Fortunately there was a farmer who had seen a rider heading for the village. When my enquiries there drew a blank I decided it was time to talk to M. Breton. I discovered he spent each afternoon at the schoolhouse, and rode on that way. Of course by the time I got there it was too late. The poor fellow was already dead in the road — but there is one point for you to consider, Miss Sedgewick: Breton had been shot in the back, a fact known only by the magistrate and myself, and, of course, the killer. I have since confirmed with Crossley that he has not mentioned the point to anyone, so how do you suppose that the *comte* learned of it?'

Madeleine put her hands over her face and drew a deep, steadying breath.

'I will not listen to this!' she cried, with a new burst of vehemence. 'Who are you, sir, to bring me such a tale. What is this matter to you? Is the government paying you, or perhaps some other party?'

'No, Miss Sedgewick, I work for no one, but my contacts in France have enabled me to be of some use to my country and I am well acquainted with the Foreign Secretary, although officially he knows nothing of my business.'

'Does Sir Thomas know why you are in his house?'

'In part, yes. I asked him to invite your party to Wyre — it was necessary to have the *comte* under surveillance, and what more natural than an invitation to stay with friends?'

'But if your suspicions are correct, Sir Thomas would be endangering his own family,' she said, aghast. 'He would not willingly do that.'

'Sir Thomas does not know why I persuaded him to invite your cousin, but he knows sufficient of me not to enquire too deeply.' His lips twitched. 'In fact, I suspect he thinks it is my growing interest in a certain young lady that prompted my request. But to be serious, I do not think the Frenchman intends to harm anyone at Wyre — except myself, of course.'

'But why should he want to kill you?'

'Perhaps because I suspect him, and possibly he knew the reason for my visit to Dorking.'

Madeleine found herself picturing her cousin in the hall at Wyre that morning. He had been standing beside one of the console tables and had she not seen the silver letter tray upon that very table?

'It makes no sense,' she said. 'If Cam — if he is an impostor, what can he hope to gain by these murders? He cannot expect to eliminate everyone who knows the *comte*.'

'He could gain time. Possibly enough to infiltrate our highest society, with your father's unwitting help. He might be aiming to assassinate some key political figure in the war, or merely to create some scandal that would undermine confidence in the government. I cannot really say. It is even possible that he looks for a suitable marriage to give him the necessary entrée.'

She flushed at the inference.

'That is a despicable thing to suggest.'

'But it could well be true.' He paused, then added gently, 'You are tired, Madeleine. We will talk further in the morning. Ah, Mrs Cubbs, you are just in time. Miss Sedgewick is wishing to retire. Perhaps you would show her to her room?'

'Most certainly, sir,' declared the good woman. She turned, smiling, to Madeleine who felt that she was being swept along by some inexorable tide.

Mr Hauxwell went to the door, holding it open for her to pass and as she went by he caught her hand.

'Sleep well, Miss Sedgewick,' he murmured, raising her fingers to his lips. 'In the morning we shall return you safely to your mama.'

'Yes. Goodnight, sir.'

She followed her hostess upstairs to a small, chilly bedroom overlooking the yard, but before preparing for bed, Madeleine checked that the window was securely fastened and she bolted the bedroom door. A few minutes later she slid between the sheets that Mrs Cubbs had thoughtfully warmed for her and lay there listening to the snores of the serving maid who was asleep on a truckle bed in the corner of the room. Despite her earlier exhaustion, Madeleine now felt wide awake with so many conflicting thoughts racing through her mind. She had just resigned herself to a long and sleepless night when weariness overtook her and she fell into a deep, dreamless sleep.

13

The morning was well advanced when Madeleine awoke. Once the memory of the past twenty-four hours returned to her she dressed hurriedly and went downstairs. When the landlord brought her breakfast he informed her that Mr Hauxwell was closeted with the squire and would join her presently. She was pouring herself a second cup of coffee when he came in, looking much bigger than she remembered, his shoulders filling the parlour doorway and he had to lower his head to avoid the lintel. He was dressed in a fresh lawn shirt, with his flowered waistcoat over it, and buckskins and top-boots that had been brushed to remove all traces of the previous day's journey. He looked more of a country gentleman than a London beau, but apart from the sling supporting his left arm, Madeleine thought he had never looked better.

'Good morning, Miss Sedgewick,' he greeted her, sketching a bow. 'I do hope you can forgive me appearing before you *en déshabillé*, but although I am grateful to our host for supplying me with a shirt last night, I cannot find it in me to accept one of his coats. We are much the same size across the shoulders, but the good fellow is a full head shorter than I. I made sure you would understand that I could not appear before you looking such a figure of fun. My surcoat will suffice for our homeward journey.'

She smiled, but in a perfunctory manner.

'The magistrate, is he still here? Does he wish to see me?'

He shook his head.

'No, you may be easy on that point, my dear. Squire Adams has gone home for his breakfast, but he knows our direction and will call at Wyre Hall should he need to see either of us at some later date.'

'Have you breakfasted sir? There is plenty here for two,' said Madeleine, relieved that she did not have to go over the events of the previous day, at least for a while.

'Thank you, but I have already eaten. You can pour me a cup of coffee, if you would.' He sat down beside her. 'I have already given orders for our horses to be saddled. I thought you would wish to be gone as soon as possible.'

'Yes. Thank you. I did not expect to sleep so long. I am sorry if I have kept you.'

'Not at all. I would have had to speak to Squire Adams in any event, so we shall not be much delayed, and the rest has done you good, Madeleine; you are looking much better this morning.'

She blushed faintly, but ignored the familiar use of her name.

'Thank you — and I also give you my thanks for sending along one of your neckcloths.' She put her hand up to the thick folds of the cravat beneath her chin, 'I feel properly dressed again now.'

'My pleasure, ma'am. I always carry a couple of spare cravats in my portmanteau. And your simple arrangement would not look out of place on any aspiring man of fashion.'

'Thank you, sir.'

Returning to more serious matters, Madeleine asked if there was any clue to Jenkins's murder.

'No one appears to have heard or seen anything.'

'What of the note that he received — is there no clue there?'

'No one has seen it. I looked for it myself yesterday and found nothing. The squire tells me his men carried out a thorough search, so we can assume the killer removed it. The landlord located the lad who delivered the note, but he was not able to give much of a description, beyond the fact that it was a man dressed in plain brown, riding a bay horse.

He could not even say for sure if the fellow was English.'

'That must be disappointing for you,' she said drily.

'Let us say it would have narrowed the field if he had spoken with a French accent.'

She finished her coffee and set the cup down with a snap.

'You persist in suspecting my cousin.'

'I do, and with your help, I could prove it.'

She regarded him with suspicion.

'How?'

'Is there some member of your family who knows the Comte du Vivière, someone who has seen him in recent years?'

'Only Cousin Charles. He visited the *comte* in Dijon last year, but he is now thought to be somewhere in Europe. It would be impossible to trace him quickly.'

'I have no wish to find him, only to use his name. I would like the *comte* to believe that this Charles is about to arrive at Wyre Hall, eager to renew his acquaintance. If the Frenchman is an impostor, he will be aware that the gentleman's appearance would reveal his disguise and he would be forced to act. I think it is improbable that he would attempt another killing, especially as he knows that I am already suspicious of him. No, it is more likely that he will try to fly the country.'

'And you want me to tell him Charles is coming to Wyre.'

'Your help would be very valuable, Miss Sedgewick.'

She rose and walked slowly to the window.

'I cannot,' she said in a strangled voice. 'I could not betray him in such a way.'

'But doubts concerning the *comte* are already in your mind, are they not?' he asked her gently. 'Do you not wish to resolve the matter? If he is indeed your cousin, and innocent, there will be no great harm done.'

She turned to face him. 'But you do not believe him innocent.'

He stood up, returning her gaze steadily. 'No, Miss Sedgewick, I do not.'

She covered her face with her hands for a moment, and when she spoke her voice was low, and angry.

'How I wish I had never met you, or Camille! I cannot, will not, deceive him.' She looked at him with stormy eyes. 'I have no reason to distrust my cousin, but you, sir, there are many reasons why I should suspect *you*! To begin with, you slip into the country in disguise, display a spurious interest in Cassandra in order to gain entry to Wyre Hall, and you had the opportunity — and for all I know the *reason* to kill Monsieur Breton!'

'But I have not killed anyone,' he replied calmly, coming towards her. 'And what is more you do not *believe* I am guilty.'

'No, but that does not mean I must suspect Camille.'

She gazed at him, her eyes imploring him to understand. He reached up and ran a finger gently along her cheek.

'Very well, my dear, I will not press you further.' He turned. 'If you have finished your meal, we can be on our way.'

'By all means.' She moved to the door. 'I have just to collect my hat and gloves and I shall be ready.' She hesitated as she passed him, looking up into his grave face. 'I am sorry, sir, but *truly* I could not — '

'You have no need to explain. Believe me, I fully understand.'

'You do?'

His eyes glinted down at her as he replied, 'Yes, I do!'

A sudden thought came to her and she said quickly, 'I am not in love with my cousin, if that is what you think.'

A smile played around the corners of his mouth, but he replied gravely, 'I am delighted to hear it, Miss Sedgewick. Shall we move on?'

★ ★ ★

231

It was very nearly midday before they finally left the inn, keeping a steady pace in deference to Mr Hauxwell's injured arm. They kept to the open ground, skirting round any areas of dense woodland that would give cover to an attacker. After a long canter, they slowed to walking pace, resting their horses, and Madeleine was anxious to know if her companion's arm was troubling him.

'No. It is a little stiff, but I expected that.'

'We must be about halfway by now,' she said. 'If you can maintain the pace we should be back at Wyre within the hour.'

'Relieved, my dear?'

'Of course, although I cannot say I look forward to the explanations.'

'You have nothing to fear, child, there will be no scandal.'

She smiled faintly. 'No, of course not.'

'It might be best if we did not mention the unfortunate Mr Jenkins — there is no need to look quite so suspiciously at me, Miss Sedgewick. I have no evil plan in mind. I shall put the matter to our host at a convenient moment, to prepare him for a visit from the magistrate, but I have no wish to increase the agitation of the other members of the party.'

'Very well, sir. It shall be as you wish, only . . . I do not think you should mention your suspicions concerning my cousin.'

'Of course not.'

He waited for her to speak again.

'What would happen to Camille if he were guilty?'

'He would be tried for murder.'

'And . . . executed?'

'Yes.'

She shuddered. 'I could not help you send a man to his death,' she whispered.

'Of course not.'

They did not speak again and very soon resumed their steady canter west towards Wyre Hall. Madeleine only broke the silence when they reached the familiar country of Sir Thomas's estate and slowed to rest her horse.

'Sir — '

'I wish you would call me Andrew.'

'Certainly not!' she retorted, shocked.

'Perhaps it might be a little unwise, after the past four-and-twenty hours, but there can be no objection to your using my name when we are alone.'

She could not suppress a chuckle.

'After the past four-and-twenty hours, as you put it, there will be little chance of that. It is far more likely that Mama will bundle me home to Stapley before I can get into any more scrapes.'

'And would one be allowed to call upon

you there, Miss Sedgewick?'

Her eyes twinkled. 'I am afraid sir,' she replied, at her most demure, 'my grandfather does not welcome guests to Stapley.'

'How uncomfortable for you.'

'It is much more uncomfortable for our visitors, I assure you.'

The gentleman considered the matter.

'Do you know,' he said at last, 'I think it would be much better if we persuaded your mama to keep you at Wyre a little longer?' He looked up. 'I see the park ahead of us. Now, do we ride direct to the house, or shall we head for the stables and attempt to approach unnoticed?'

'We shall take the main drive, naturally,' returned Madeleine, putting up her chin. 'We have nothing to hide.'

'Good girl!' he said approvingly, and earned a withering look from his companion.

'I am not your girl!'

'That could be arranged, my dear.'

'Is that a proposal?'

He met her challenging stare with a bland smile.

'Would you like me to offer for you?'

She coloured hotly. 'Not at all!' she flashed. 'I wish you would put such an idiotic idea out of your head! One moment you accuse my cousin of the most heinous crimes and the next — it is most improper!'

'Very well, Miss Sedgewick, if that is what you wish,' he said meekly.

'In any event,' said Madeleine, after they had ridden in silence for a few minutes, 'after what has occurred it would give rise to some very ugly rumours.'

'Quite so,' agreed her companion. 'Far better to wait until this episode has blown over before we make any announcement. What do you consider a suitable period?'

'I think that we had best stop this conversation,' she replied unsteadily. 'I have no wish to marry anyone!'

'That is very strange. I had not thought of you as old maidish, but perhaps you know best — after all you do have a tendency to get as cross as crabs over nothing — '

'How dare you!' she exclaimed, her eyes blazing.

'You see my point, you are again firing up at me for no reason.'

'You are abominable!' she threw at him. 'I would not marry you if you were the last man on earth!'

She spurred Amber on, but soon found the black alongside her.

'If I were that, my dear,' he called to her, 'it would be most inconsiderate of you to do so!'

Madeleine tried to suppress her emotions, but despite her efforts a bubble of laughter escaped her.

Her eyes were still dancing when they reached the house, but her good humour soon abated when she saw her mother's strained and anxious countenance as that lady ran out of the house to meet her.

'Oh Maddie, thank heaven you are safe! I feared some dreadful accident!'

Miss Sedgewick slipped from the saddle and embraced her mama.

'No, I am quite safe, I assure you,' she said unsteadily. 'I am grieved to have been the cause of so much worry. Indeed, we did try to send a message to you last night, but it was so dark.'

'Let us go inside, my love, and you can tell me. Sir Thomas and the other gentlemen are out now, scouring the countryside, but the ladies are gathered in the drawing-room, and very anxious for news.' Mrs Sedgewick broke off and looked uncertainly towards Mr Hauxwell. 'If you would prefer to talk to me in private, Madeleine.'

'No, no, Mama. Let us join the others. One explanation will serve for all.' She turned to Mr Hauxwell, feeling suddenly a little shy. 'Will you come with us, sir?'

He gave a bow of acquiescence and

escorted the two ladies to the drawing-room, where their entrance caused a sudden flurry of activity.

Cassandra flew across the room to hug her friend, while the other ladies gathered around, full of concern and with curious side-glances towards Mr Hauxwell, who had unbuttoned his greatcoat to display his injured arm reposing in its sling.

'Oh Madeleine, I have been in agony waiting for news. You must tell us everything,' cried Miss Wyre, clinging to her hand. 'When Kilmer and I came back yesterday and found you had not arrived — I vow I have not slept all night. I should never have let you go off alone . . . '

'Cassandra, hush dearest, and let Madeleine speak,' Lady Wyre gently admonished her daughter, then she smiled at Miss Sedgewick. 'We are all curious to know what happened, but if you do not wish to talk, so be it, we shall not press you.'

'Oh I am quite happy to tell you, ma'am.'

Madeleine took a seat beside her mother, while Cassandra dropped down upon a low stool at her feet and the other ladies made themselves comfortable around them, Mrs Eldwick shepherding her own young ladies to a vacant sofa at a safe distance from Mr Hauxwell, whose presence she viewed with deep suspicion, a feeling evidently not shared by her daughters.

'I wonder if Mr Hauxwell will tell us how he injured his arm,' put in Miss Eldwick loudly.

'All in good time, Phoebe,' her mother frowned. 'Let Miss Sedgewick tell us her story first.'

'Perhaps he was wounded saving Miss Sedgewick from some wicked attacker,' suggested the younger Miss Eldwick, her eyes shining.

The gentleman smiled. 'On the contrary, it was Miss Sedgewick who saved *me* from a highway robber.'

All eyes turned back to Madeleine, who coloured faintly. She looked at Mr Hauxwell.

'Sir, would it not be best if you were to explain?'

'No, Miss Sedgewick. I am sure your audience would prefer to hear the story from your own lips.'

Slowly, Madeleine gave them the barest details of her chance meeting with Mr Hauxwell and their madcap race across country. She cast an apologetic glance at her mother.

'Once I had done my best to bind up Mr Hauxwell's arm, there was less than two hours of daylight left. We could not get back to Wyre before dark, so we carried on to Dorking and put up at the Lion.' Observing her mama's anxious countenance, she added, 'I asked the landlord if we could get a message to you, but the rain had set in and he thought it impossible for anyone to find their way in the darkness.'

'Very true,' affirmed Cassandra. 'The *comte* missed dinner last night because he had been out riding and missed his way.'

Madeleine felt Mr Hauxwell's eyes upon her and it was as much as she could do to keep from looking at him.

'So you passed the night at the Lion in Dorking,' prompted Mrs Sedgewick, her vinaigrette in her hand.

Madeleine squeezed her hand reassuringly.

'Yes. Mr Hauxwell was very good — he took care of everything, and even arranged for a serving maid to attend me. I passed a very tolerable night — indeed, I feel a little ashamed to think I slept so soundly, when you were all so worried.'

Mrs Sedgewick clasped her daughter to her.

'You are safe now, my love. That is all that matters to me.'

'What an adventure!' declared Miss Wyre. 'Oh how I wish I had been with you!'

'You could have had my part in it, with my

good will!' retorted her friend, laughing. 'I am sorry I have put everyone to so much trouble. When do you expect Sir Thomas to return, Lady Wyre?'

'The gentlemen should be back by dusk: and you are not to be thinking that Sir Thomas and the others will consider their time has been wasted. When they hear your story they will be only too thankful that you have come back safely — and you too, Mr Hauxwell,' added my lady. 'What a dreadful thing to happen. I do hope you are not seriously hurt? We will send for Dr Tibbs if you require — '

'No, ma'am, I thank you. The bullet passed straight through without doing too much damage. All I need is to keep it still for a few more days. However, I will have my man put a fresh bandage on it. If you will excuse me, ma'am, I should like to retire to my room and make myself a little more presentable before dinner.'

'Yes, of course, sir,' beamed my lady. 'What a pleasant gentleman,' she added, when he had gone out, 'and what a lucky thing you chanced upon him, Madeleine, or goodness knows but the villains might have gone after him.'

'A lucky thing!' repeated Mrs Eldwick in astonishment. 'Surely, my lady. it would have been better if she had come home with Miss Wyre and Lord Kilmer. It is most improper to go riding off alone!'

'Well, at least my child is safely returned,' put in Mrs Sedgewick. 'One could wish it had been possible for you to get back to Wyre last night, my love, but there it is! Heaven knows what your father will say when he hears of this on Monday.'

Madeleine turned to her mother, her attention caught.

'He is coming for certain? You have had word?'

'Why yes, my love. I received a short note from him this very morning, so barring bad weather your papa will be with us again the day after tomorrow.'

'Oh that is the best news I could wish to hear!' cried Madeleine, 'There are — certain matters I want to discuss with him. But I will not bore you with that, Mama. Instead I shall follow Mr Hauxwell's example and go away to make myself more presentable.'

As she rose from her seat, the faint sound of voices could be heard and hasty footsteps approached the drawing-room. Then Sir Thomas appeared in the doorway.

'Aha!' he cried, striding into the room, 'So here is our elusive lady!' he held out his arms and Madeleine ran forward to be enveloped

241

in Sir Thomas's warm and none-too-gentle embrace.

'My dear child.' He held her at arm's length, subjecting her to a frowning scrutiny. 'We were all imagining that you had met with some horrible accident, perhaps lying in a ditch somewhere with your neck broken, and here you are looking prettier than ever. And don't tell me that I've creased your gown, because if a man can't hug his own god-daughter then things have come to a pretty pass!'

'I would not think of telling you any such thing, sir,' she laughed at him.

'We did not expect you to return for a good while yet, Sir Thomas,' put in his lady.

'We were circling back towards Ewhurst when we heard that a young woman fitting Maddie's description had been seen earlier today, riding in this direction with a gentle-man. We were persuaded to return home, to see if by some happy chance it was our own dear Madeleine returned to us, and I learn at the door that you rode in with Hauxwell.'

'Yes, sir, and I must beg your forgiveness for being the cause of so much concern — '

'Think no more about it, Miss Sedgewick,' said Lord Kilmer, who had followed his host into the room. 'We would not grudge ten times the trouble.'

'Oh quite so, ma'am,' agreed Mr Fulbeck, coming up to take her hand. 'But how comes it that you rode back with Andrew? I thought he was in Dorking.'

'Oh, it is a tedious long story,' she replied vaguely, her eyes fixed upon the door, but after Mr Eldwick had come in, the footman retired, closing the door firmly behind him. Madeleine turned to Sir Thomas with a faint crease between her brows.

'Where is the *comte*, sir? Did he not ride with you?'

'Aye he did, but I fear our slow search was not to his liking and he rode off to cover some extra ground.' He observed her anxious look and added, 'I sent Westlake and a groom along with him, so there is no fear he will miss his way home!'

Mr Eldwick chuckled.

'The lad could hardly wait to be away this morning, so eager was he to be looking for you, Miss Sedgewick!' He winked and added slyly, 'He is showing all the signs of a young man in love, ain't that so, Sir Thomas? But don't you worry, Miss Sedgewick, we sent a man out after 'em, as soon as we arrived here and knew you was safe — don't want the *comte* to be searching all night for you, as I've no doubt he would do!'

'Enough of all this nonsense,' put in Sir

243

Thomas, waving his hand dismissively. 'we all want to know what happened to you, my girl!'

Madeleine quickly ran through the details of her adventure, making no demur when Cassandra told her father that Mr Hauxwell had been attacked by highwaymen. At length, having completed her tale for the second time, she was able to get away and hurried to her own room, her spirits lifted by the knowledge that her father would soon be at Wyre Hall. She would lay before him all her doubts and fears concerning the events of the past few days and she was confident he would know what to do.

★　★　★

When Madeleine entered the drawing-room it wanted but ten minutes to the dinner hour and as she expected, the guests were all assembled, including the *comte*. He came forward to meet her, catching her hands and raising them to his lips.

'Ah, Cousin, what happiness it gives me to see you. You cannot imagine my torment for these past days. When I heard this afternoon that you were here, safe, I returned with all speed.'

She answered him coolly, hoping that she did not look as uncomfortable as she felt, for although she had rejected Mr Hauxwell's suspicions concerning the *comte*, she could not completely dispel them, even though her thoughts made her feel wretchedly deceitful. However, at dinner, she found herself sitting next to her cousin and his manner towards her was so solicitous that her doubts subsided and she began to relax. When the covers had been removed and the servants withdrawn, the conversation turned naturally to what was coming to be known as Miss Sedgewick's Adventure.

'If only I had insisted that you come back with us,' remarked Cassandra. 'I shall never forgive myself for allowing you to ride off alone into such danger.'

'Oh, I think I had very little to fear,' replied Madeleine, trying to reassure her friend. 'My main concern was to get back to Wyre as quickly as possible — I knew you would be worried for me.'

'Forgive me, my knowledge of the country is not great,' said the *comte*, 'but why did you make for Dorking? That would take you away from Wyre, I think?'

'It was the nearest town of any size,' she replied. 'We could be sure of accommodation there, and a doctor for Mr Hauxwell, although once the landlady had cleaned the wound we found it was not so bad after all, and Mr Hauxwell would not let us send for a doctor.'

The Frenchman looked across the table at Mr Hauxwell, who was idly studying his wineglass.

'A lucky escape for you, sir, but did I not hear that you were in fact bound for Dorking yesterday?

'That is correct, Monsieur le Comte, but unfortunately, my acquaintance had already left the place when we arrived. Given me up, I daresay, for it was growing very late by then. Which reminds me, *m'sieur*, did you not have a little trouble yourself, yesterday evening, finding your way home?'

Madeleine held her breath, but the *comte* showed no signs of discomfort.

'Yes, I rode over to see Madame Breton — to offer what little assistance was in my power, you understand. Her plight so distressed me, I could not return here immediately. Instead I rode for a mile or two, until my spirits were more composed. But to find my way back — I thought I should be forced to sleep in a field, it grew so black, and the rain too, made it very uncomfortable.'

From across the table Cassandra nodded.

'I wanted Papa to send out a searching party for you last night, Maddie, but when the *comte* told us how dark it was, Papa said

246

it would be useless.'

'Well, I am back now, and no harm done,' replied Miss Sedgewick, wishing to conclude the subject. 'I think it is time we turned our attention away from the past, and concentrated upon the happier events to come.'

'Hear, hear!' applauded Sir Thomas. 'There is Cassie's engagement to Lord Kilmer to be arranged; it is to be announced at Christmas and I've no doubt the ladies will be wanting another tiresome party.'

'Fie on you, Papa, do not tease us so,' cried Cassandra. 'Of course we want a ball, and you would not have it otherwise.'

He chuckled at her indignant face.

'As you wish, my love, but before that there is a treat in store for Madeleine, is there not, ma'am?' He turned to Mrs Sedgewick, whose gentle face lit up with a smile.

'Oh yes, sir, indeed there is. In all the excitement today, I quite forgot to mention to anyone save Sir Thomas that your Papa will be bringing someone with him to Wyre on Monday — my cousin Charles!'

14

For a long moment Madeleine could only stare at her mama.

'He — he is?' she managed to say at last.

'Yes, is it not wonderful news?'

'Wonderful,' murmured Miss Sedgewick faintly.

'It will be an opportunity for you to renew your acquaintance with my cousin Charles, Camille,' continued Mrs Sedgewick, smiling at the *comte*, 'and in happier circumstances than when you last met in Dijon. Your uncle writes that he has asked after you.'

The *comte* raised his glass, smiling.

'I am honoured that he should remember me. I drink to his safe arrival on Monday.'

The ladies soon withdrew but Madeleine found it impossible to settle to any occupation, her thoughts once again in turmoil. When the gentlemen came into the drawing-room she lost no time in seeking a quiet word with Mr Hauxwell.

'Is this your doing, sir?' she asked him bluntly. 'This supposed visit of Mama's cousin?'

'Not at all. I was as surprised as you to hear of it.'

'No doubt it suits your plans admirably,' she retorted, bitterly.

He patted the sling which supported his left arm.

'I would prefer to have the use of this before a confrontation, but Fate, it seems, decrees otherwise.'

'Perhaps Fate will prove you are mistaken,' she replied. 'I cannot think Camille is dangerous.'

His thoughtful gaze rested on her for a moment.

''*She fear'd no danger, for she knew no sin*',' he quoted softly.

Madeleine flushed.

'Perhaps, sir, there is some '*green-eyed monster*' that prevents *you* from seeing things clearly!' she threw at him as she walked away.

★　★　★

Despite a very tiring day, Madeleine found sleep eluded her. She lay awake long into the night, at one point even jumping from her bed and running to the window when she heard a faint sound, half expecting to see some shadowy figure riding away across the park in the moonlight. However, there was nothing and Madeleine lay down again, angrily admonishing herself for being so fanciful. Resolutely she pulled the blankets up around her ears and eventually fell into a fitful slumber. When morning came at last, she made her way slowly downstairs and her relief when she saw the *comte* making his way to the breakfast room was almost overwhelming.

Being a Sunday, the carriages were soon at the door, waiting to take Sir Thomas and his guests to the tiny church in the village.

'Your cousin does not come with us?' enquired Mr Hauxwell, as he handed Madeleine into her seat.

'I would not expect him to do so, since he is a Catholic.'

'Such a pity about that,' remarked Mrs Sedgewick, settling herself into a corner. 'I have no doubt it would comfort the poor young man to hear the scriptures. They give one such solace, do you not agree, Mr Hauxwell?'

The gentleman had followed Madeleine into the coach and made himself comfortable on the forward seat, facing the ladies.

'Oh yes, ma'am,' he agreed, 'I have often said so myself.'

'Perhaps the text for today will be St Matthew,' observed Miss Sedgewick meaningfully, '*Judge not, that ye be not judged*'.'

He met her gaze coolly.

'My mind turns more towards Genesis: '*Whoso sheddeth man's blood, by man shall his blood be shed*'.'

Mrs Sedgewick listened to this interchange in bewilderment.

'Well, I do not pretend to understand the two of you,' she said at last, 'but I must say, sir, that I hope the parson will have something a little more cheerful than that for us today. With Madeleine safely restored to me, and my dear Mr Sedgewick coming here tomorrow, I cannot find it in me to be so serious.' Her bright eyes glanced from her daughter to the gentleman. 'A quiet little sermon on the blessings of matrimony could be quite in order, I think — in view of Miss Wyre's coming betrothal!' she continued hastily, as Madeleine turned an outraged countenance towards her.

Mr Hauxwell looked to be much amused by this little speech, but wisely decided to remain silent. Later, when they had finished their devotions, he used his considerable charm to coax Miss Sedgewick into a sunnier mood. He succeeded very well, and the fact that the *comte* was waiting for their return to beg the honour of Madeleine's company for a quiet stroll in the gardens added the final lift to her spirits. She stole a glance at her cousin's profile as they walked. Surely no impostor could look quite so composed if he were about to be unmasked. Becoming aware of her scrutiny, Camille turned his head and smiled at her.

'You are frowning at me, *ma chère*. Have I offended you?'

'No, Cousin. My thoughts were elsewhere,' she responded with an answering smile.

'With another gentleman, perhaps?'

'Of course not.'

He observed the flush on her cheeks and said slowly, 'It was my intention to speak to your father upon a certain matter — no, Madeleine, please do not speak. As I was saying, I intended to talk to my uncle about a closer alliance between our two houses, which I know at one time was the wish of both our mothers.'

'When we were babes, perhaps, but — '

He held up his hand to silence her interruption.

'Undoubtedly when we were infants. Since my arrival in England I have developed a very great regard for you, Madeleine, but, my dear, I fear you do not return my affection.' He paused, then continued with a small, sad smile, 'Your silence gives me my answer, Cousin.'

'I am sorry if it pains you, Camille,' she said quietly. 'I have never knowingly encouraged you to hope — '

'No, no, I lay no blame at your door. It is sad for me, but not unexpected. I merely wished to clarify the matter.' He stopped and raised her hand to his lips. 'There, it is over. Pray do not look so sad, my pretty one, I shall not refer to the matter again, I promise you, but it is better that we understand each other.'

'Very true, Camille. I am pleased to have settled the point, for now we may be easy.'

★   ★   ★

Going upstairs to change out of her walking dress some time later, Madeleine felt another burden had been lifted from her shoulders. With their conversation in the garden, Camille had removed a problem that had been worrying her and his obvious lack of concern over the imminent arrival of Cousin Charles laid to rest her doubts about his identity. Tomorrow she would see her father again and he would assure her that she had been worrying unnecessarily, she was sure of it. With her spirits soaring, she turned away from her more sober gowns and chose instead an overdress of rose silk with a matching glazed wool petticoat and little silk slippers. She allowed her maid to arrange her hair in soft curls about her face, but she waved away the rouge pot. Thirty minutes before dinner she made her way to the drawing-room, looking forward to a pleasant evening. She entered to find most of the party already assembled. She spotted the *comte* standing to one side of the room and she smiled at him but did not approach, moving instead towards her mother, who was sitting by the fire. Mr Hauxwell bowed to her as she approached.

'You look very well this evening, Miss Sedgewick, perhaps I should say triumphant?'

'Relieved would be a better word, sir. I am glad in this instance to prove you wrong about my cousin.'

'I, too, would be glad if you could do so,' he murmured, stepping aside to let her pass.

Madeleine decided she would avoid both gentlemen as much as possible this evening, and remained with her mama who periodically turned to her daughter and squeezed her hand, as if reassuring herself that Madeleine was indeed safe.

There was a mood of gaiety and celebration in the house that evening: the guests were all in high spirits and several were persuaded to display their musical abilities. Cassandra and Lord Kilmer, apparently unwilling to be separated even for the duration of a song, performed a duet, their voices blending so admirably that Lady Wyre was forced to wipe away a tear. Madeleine took her seat at the pianoforte to play a couple of Irish airs then returned to her mother's side while the Eldwick girls displayed their talents. The *comte* took an empty chair beside her, whispering his compliments on her performance.

'Thank you, Cousin, but I lack practice. When we return to Stapley I shall look out the music for a series of French songs — I would like to play them for you.'

'How kind of you — I would like that, *ma chère*.' He clasped her hand briefly. 'What time do you expect your father to return tomorrow?'

'I have no idea, although knowing Papa he will most likely set out early, to be with us as soon as possible.' She looked up at him anxiously. 'Camille, you are not — you have no worries over meeting Cousin Charles tomorrow?'

He looked at her in surprise, then his dark eyes glowed with amusement.

'None at all, Cousin! What a strange thought — but I know who has put this suspicion into your mind.' He glanced across the room towards Mr Hauxwell. 'You may be assured, Cousin, I have no worries at all for the morrow.'

'I am very glad of it, Camille.'

He smiled, raising her fingers to his lips.

'You have been very anxious for me, have you not? But you may rest easy, Madeleine. There will be no problem tomorrow, and you need not worry for me ever again.'

★ ★ ★

It was past midnight when the party broke up and Madeleine made her way upstairs alone, looking forward to the prospect of a good night's sleep. Her hopes were not to be realized, for hardly had she sat down at her mirror to take off her pearls than there was a faint scratching at the door and Cassandra peeped into the room, a silk wrap covering her nightdress.

'Maddie? Oh good, you are not abed yet. I saw you come up, but I had to let Lizzie take away my dress for brushing before I could come and find you.'

'Do you wish to talk, Cassie?'

'Of course!' cried Miss Wyre. 'Pray do not tell me you are tired, Maddie. Send your maid to bed and come to my room,' she said coaxingly. 'I have scarce had a chance to talk to you since Friday. I will not keep you long, I promise.'

Realizing that it would require more effort

to argue than to assent, Madeleine dismissed her maid and followed Cassandra into the corridor.

'Very well, Cassie, I will come with you, but for only five minutes.'

'You are a darling.' Cassandra smiled happily. 'You had best borrow one of my wraps to put around you, for my fire has gone out, and as I told Lizzie not to come back tonight, there is no one to make it up again.'

'Then why do we not stay in my room?'

She received only a mischievous look in reply.

'We will be comfortable enough.' Cassandra ushered her friend into her room and closed the door. Madeleine made herself comfortable upon one corner of the bed while Cassandra found an old grey cloak to wrap around her, to ward off the growing chill in the air.

'Now Cassie, tell me what you are about!' demanded Madeleine.

Miss Wyre did not answer, but went over to one of her cupboards and produced a bottle and two glasses. Madeleine stared at her.

'Champagne! Cassie, what is that doing here?'

'I smuggled it upstairs,' giggled Cassandra. 'For our own little celebration.'

After a brief struggle with the cork

Cassandra poured out the bubbling liquid, then climbed upon the bed and handed Miss Sedgewick a glass.

'Kilmer and I are to be married; you are safely home again: is that not worthy of a toast?'

'Yes, I suppose it is, but pray do not spill wine all over the counterpane.'

Solemnly they raised their glasses and saluted one another.

Miss Sedgewick sipped at her champagne, then laughed.

'I have not done this sort of thing since my schooldays.'

'Nor I, but with my betrothal to Kilmer so close, I fear I shall soon be entering another kind of life: I will be obliged to grow up then.'

'Is this then a final girlish prank?' smiled Madeleine.

'In a way. I wish we were celebrating your betrothal too.'

'Oh? Who had you in mind for me?'

'Well, I thought for a while it would be your handsome French cousin, but I have returned to my original choice: Mr Hauxwell will do very nicely for you.'

'And how, pray, did you reach that conclusion?'

Cassandra considered the matter.

'It is the eyes,' she decided at last. 'When

the two of you are together, you seem to share some private joke — it shows itself in your laughing eyes. Why, even this evening, when you scarce spoke to each other, I noted that you were forever exchanging glances.'

Miss Sedgewick was so much surprised by this sudden burst of perspicacity from her young friend that she could think of nothing to say, but hearing a clock somewhere chime the hour she jumped up.

'Two o'clock — gracious, I must go!'

'Oh not yet, Maddie. Please stay a little longer, we have scarce drunk half the bottle yet.'

'I certainly do not intend to help you finish it tonight!'

'Just one more glass, for the passing of our childhood.'

Miss Sedgewick was obliged to smile at this.

'Very well, but only one glass,' she relented. 'Then I mean to go to my room and sleep.'

Miss Wyre refilled the glasses and the young ladies took their ease upon the bed, enjoying a prolonged and lively conversation until at length Madeleine resolutely drained her glass and went across the room to set it down upon the dressing-table.

'Now I really must go,' she said. 'Lord Kilmer will not thank me for chattering with you through the night, especially if you appear at breakfast with unseemly shadows beneath your eyes.'

'Oh very well, if you must. I suppose the rest of this must be wasted.' Cassandra reluctantly set down the half-empty bottle.

'I suppose it will,' replied Madeleine evenly. 'What are you going to do with the bottle and glasses?'

'I must take them back to the drawing-room: the servants will clear them away in the morning without any questions.'

'Let me take them for you,' offered Madeleine. 'I am still wearing my gown, which will occasion a great deal less comment than your nightgown, should there be anyone on the stairs.'

The offer was gratefully accepted and Madeleine crept into the corridor, being very careful not to let the glasses chink together. It was Sir Thomas's custom to have night-lights burning throughout the main passages and stairways of the house when he was in residence and Madeleine was relieved the necessity of taking a candle with her. The rustle of her skirts seemed abnormally loud as she made her way down the stairs and across the inner hall to the drawing-room. She realized she was still wearing Cassandra's grey wool cloak about her shoulders and was glad of its warmth on her bare shoulders.

* * *

The drawing-room was in darkness, but there was sufficient moonlight shining in through the windows for her to avoid tripping over the furniture and she placed the wine-glasses and the bottle carefully upon the side table without mishap.

Miss Sedgewick was by no means a fanciful young lady, and the darkened room did not frighten her; indeed she liked the stillness of the night and she went to the long windows that looked out over the terrace and stood quietly for some minutes, enjoying the unusual night-time view of the park and gardens. The rain clouds had broken up to allow the moon and a great many stars to display their light and she was in hopes that the spell of dry weather might last over the Christmas period. A sudden movement caught her eye and brought her out of her reverie. She shifted her gaze towards the outer wall of the stable block, which was visible from the drawing-room windows, set back behind the east wing of the house. There was no mistaking a figure moving stealthily along the wall and, as she watched, it

261

disappeared through a side door.

Without a second thought, Madeleine slipped back the bolts of the long window and stepped out on to the terrace. Seconds later she was running towards the stables. She reached the side door where the figure had disappeared and stopped there to regain her breath. She tried the handle and the door opened easily, silently. Madeleine slipped inside and found herself in the coach house. It was very dark, but a grey square of light showed her a doorway and she crept towards it, Cassandra's cloak pulled close about her to cover the shiny silk gown beneath. The aperture led through to one part of the stables and, at the far end of a row of stalls, the door leading into the yard stood open, allowing a shaft of moonlight to enter the building. Cautiously she moved towards the door and peeped out. The yard was lit by a couple of lamps burning brightly in their high wall brackets and by their light someone was harnessing a pair of horses to one of Sir Thomas's curricles. She wondered vaguely why none of the grooms had put in an appearance, but at that moment the figure moved around the horses, checking the leathers, and she had a clear view of his face.

'Camille!' She stifled the name, her heart beating fast as she feared he had heard her, but the noise of the team moving restlessly in their harness covered any slight sound she had made and she drew back into the shadows, wondering what to do. Then a familiar voice brought her back to the doorway.

'A little late to be commencing a journey is it not, Monsieur le Comte?'

Mr Hauxwell had appeared on the far side of the stable yard and from her own position Madeleine had a clear view of him and of the *comte*, who was standing beside the curricle.

'Have you come to bid me *adieu*, Hauxwell?' enquired the Frenchman calmly, throwing his travelling bag into the curricle.

'Perhaps. How tiresome that you were obliged to put the horses to. Where are the stable boys?'

'Drugged. A state which you should envy them, *m'sieur*.' He produced a pistol and levelled it at Mr Hauxwell, who remained facing him, the pale lamplight gleaming on the white sling on his left arm.

'Well, why not shoot me? Surely you do not hesitate over one more murder?'

'No — Andrew!'

Madeleine ran out from her hiding place then stopped, realizing her folly. The *comte* smiled at her, his pistol never wavering from its target.

'Ah, good evening, *ma chère*. You are in good time to be of service. Come, Madeleine, close to me, if you do not wish me to put a bullet in your friend.'

'Should that not be *another* bullet, *m'sieur*?'

'Ah but of course — you are right, Hauxwell, as ever.'

'I-I do not understand,' faltered Madeleine, stepping closer to the *comte*.

'Perhaps you should explain yourself, Monsieur le Comte — or should we call you Monsieur Menotte?' drawled Mr Hauxwell.

The Frenchman shrugged. 'Monsieur le Comte is my correct title. I inherit it from my cousin.'

'You — you are not Camille? Where is he? What have you done with him?' demanded Madeleine.

'He is dead, my dear. Alas, I do not know what became of his body.'

She stared at him, horrified.

'And . . . and Monsieur Breton?'

'*Oui*. Him also did I kill.'

'But, why?'

'To buy time. Time to establish myself in London, perhaps.'

'And what did you propose to do there?' put in Mr Hauxwell, stepping forward.

'You will remain where you are, Hauxwell!

I do not know what I might have achieved. An assassination, perhaps some minister, or even the Prince of Wales. Who knows? My cousin's intention of coming to England, his impeccable family connections here — it was too good an opportunity to miss. I might have succeeded in helping my country to victory.'

Madeleine gasped. 'But you could not get away with such a scheme — you would be caught.'

'My life is not important, it is for France. In any event my success or failure is nothing: we shall soon overthrow your weak, pleasure-loving leaders and return England to the people. Already they applaud us — '

'A handful of half-crazed extremists,' retorted Hauxwell.

'Such things have been said before, in Paris, where I shall now return.'

'Oh no, Comte. You do not escape that easily,' replied Mr Hauxwell coolly. 'If you will but look up to the window behind you, you will observe my groom is there with a shotgun. You will not get very far.'

'You are lying — all the stable hands are sleeping out their drunken stupor.'

'Unfortunately for you, *m'sieur*, Stebson is a strict observer of the Lord's Day. He drinks nothing stronger than small beer on Sundays, so he passed by your present of a keg of rum for the stable hands.'

The *comte*'s lips compressed into a thin line. He caught Madeleine's wrist and pulled her close to him, pressing the pistol into her side, then he glanced up towards the window, where the grey-haired groom could be seen with a long barrelled shotgun at his side.

'Very fortunate for you, Hauxwell, but I do not believe you will risk Miss Sedgewick's life.'

The gentleman stepped forward a pace, drawing his own blue-barrelled pistol from inside the sling.

'If you harm her, you villain, you will surely not live to see the dawn!'

'Very gallant, sir, but her fate is in your hands now.' The *comte* stepped into the curricle, keeping his pistol aimed at Madeleine.

'My dear, if you please — and do not think, because you are a woman, that I would hesitate to shoot you.'

She paused, looking towards Mr Hauxwell, who nodded at her. Silently she climbed up into the curricle.

'I assume Jenkins also was your work?' remarked Mr Hauxwell, coming closer.

'You refer to the man at Dorking? So you know what became of him. You are very clever, Mr Hauxwell.'

'You are very careless, sir. How far do you expect to get?'

'To the coast. I can travel for a long time without sleep, I assure you, and with Madeleine as my hostage, it is not impossible that I shall get to France.'

The lady turned to stare at him, her eyes blazing.

'You would have married me, to gain entrance into society?'

'But of course, my dear. Not that duty is always without its pleasant side.'

'You tricked me!' she accused him, her voice tight with anger, 'You deceived us all!'

'It was necessary, *ma chère*. But we delay here too long.' He picked up the reins with his free hand.

'Wait!' Hauxwell came up to the curricle. 'Let her go — if you need a hostage, take me instead.'

The *comte* laughed, a soft, menacing laugh that sent a cold shiver of fear through Madeleine.

'I think not. I am quite happy with my companion.' He held out the reins to her. 'I remember you telling me that you like to drive, Madeleine.'

'No.'

He laid the cold steel of the gun barrel

against her cheek. 'It would be a pity to spoil such a lovely face,' he murmured. 'Let us go.'

Madeleine did not move. She was ice cold now, her fury absolute.

'Madeleine, do as he says,' Hauxwell advised her sharply. 'You may be sure I shall not rest until you are safe again.'

'No. You may shoot me if you wish, Cam — Comte, but I will not help you.'

For perhaps half a minute no one moved. Madeleine closed her eyes, the rim of the barrel still pressed against her face. Then she heard again the *comte's* soft laugh. 'Oh, Madeleine, you . . . you sorceress!'

She braced herself for the shot, but instead she found herself being thrust violently out of the curricle as the *comte* whipped up the horses and galloped out of the stable yard. She was thrown against Mr Hauxwell, and they both crashed to the ground. Even as Madeleine picked herself up there was a loud retort, a scream of pain from one of the horses and the curricle slewed round, crashing on to its side just beyond the gates. Stebson disappeared from the upstairs window and seconds later was in the yard and the three of them ran out to the curricle. In the moonlight, they could see the still form of one of the horses, while the other kicked and struggled frantically to free itself from the wreckage.

'Reckon the shot passed over Frenchie's head and hit t'horse.' muttered the groom, running over to free its frenzied partner.

Madeleine's eyes strained in the darkness.

'Camille! Where is he?'

Mr Hauxwell moved forward.

'Over here.' he dropped to one knee beside the figure lying ominously still at the side of the road, then jumped up to catch Miss Sedgewick with his good arm as she came up.

'I must see him!'

'It's too late,' he said, holding her tightly, 'his neck is broken. He's dead.'

For a full minute she stood motionless, then as the rigidity left her, she crumpled against him in a dead faint.

15

After the cheerful luxury of Wyre Hall, the drawing-room at Stapley was depressing and, to Miss Sedgewick's prejudiced eye, even the fire had a sullen glow about it. They had been home for just ten days, but now Wyre seemed a lifetime away. Mr Sedgewick was engaged in a game of chess with Sir Joseph, who was so critical of every move that Madeleine wondered why her father consented to play at all. The two ladies were busy with more domestic duties, mending torn bed-linen. It was tedious work, but at least it allowed them to sit in reasonable comfort beside the fire. Miss Sedgewick looked up from her task to find her mother's eyes upon her, shining with gentle amusement.

'You have not set a stitch for the past ten minutes, Maddie. If you are tired, there is more than an hour before dinner, if you care to rest.'

'I was merely daydreaming, Mama. I am not tired.'

'Thinking of your fine friends at Wyre Hall, I don't doubt!' put in Sir Joseph acidly. 'I don't know why you bothered to come back, miss, since all you seem to enjoy is pleasuring your life away!'

'How could any of us stay after the tragic events that occurred?' demanded Mrs Sedgewick, bristling in defence of her young, 'It was bad enough that we should have introduced the *comte* to Wyre Hall, and our staying on would most surely have thrown a cloud over the celebrations for young Cassandra's betrothal.'

'Aye, madam, so you bring your melancholy back home with you! It's not enough that my family is involved in a series of murders committed by some masquerading Frenchman, but you bring my granddaughter back looking so hagged I hardly recognize her.'

Appreciating there was a degree of genuine concern in his tirade, Madeleine swallowed her retort, and listened to her father say in his mild way, 'After learning that our true nephew was indeed dead, sir, it would not have been fitting for us to join in any festivities.'

Ignoring his remarks, Sir Joseph banged his fist on the table, making the figures on the chessboard rattle nervously.

'Don't put your bishop there, idiot. You have exposed your queen. Take it back.'

Flustered, Mr Sedgewick tried again, but

this time his efforts met with even less approval, as Sir Joseph got up from the table and swept all the pieces on to the floor with his stick.

'Bah! It is useless to try to play with you — imbecile!' He would have continued to berate his son but the entrance of a wooden-faced servant cut him short, and he contented himself with swearing under his breath as the footman announced a visitor.

'Mr Andrew Hauxwell, sir.'

'Hauxwell, my dear fellow!' Mr Sedgwick got up off his knees, clutching several hapless pawns in his fingers. He put the pieces down upon the board and came forward to wring the newcomer's hand with genuine warmth. 'This is an unexpected pleasure.'

He presented the gentleman to Sir Joseph, who responded with a frosty glare. Mr Hauxwell's glance took in the scattered chess set, but without the flicker of an eyelid he went on to greet Mrs Sedgewick, who had risen from her seat and come forward to give him her fingers.

'My dear sir, you are most welcome.'

'Thank you, ma'am. When we last spoke at Wyre you were kind enough to tell me I might call and take pot-luck with you.'

'But of course! I shall have another place set for you immediately. You will of course allow us to have the pleasure of your company until tomorrow? A room can be prepared for you in an instant.'

He smiled. 'It is very fortunate that I have my portmanteau with me, Mrs Sedgewick.'

The lady's eyes twinkled responsively.

'Then I shall arrange everything, sir, while you warm yourself after your journey.'

From her place by the fire, Madeleine smiled warmly at the gentleman as he approached.

'Your arm is now fully recovered, sir?'

'As you see, I am no longer impeded by a sling. Which in part explains why I am here. I was determined not to call upon you until — ' He broke off as Mr Sedgewick came over with a glass of wine for his guest.

'Until?' she prompted him, intrigued.

The gentleman shook his head, his eyes teasing her.

'I will explain later, Miss Sedgewick.'

'So tell us, sir, how you left everyone at Wyre,' commanded Mr Sedgewick jovially, 'Have they decided upon a date to announce the betrothal?'

'Lady Wyre is holding a New Year's Ball, which I believe is now almost a tradition at Wyre, and the announcement is to be made then. By the by, her ladyship has charged me to say that she is still hopeful you might be persuaded to attend.'

'Well, well, who knows but what we might put in an appearance, if only for a short time. Although of course' — here he bent a frowning eye upon his daughter — 'with the recent loss of our nephew, I think that dancing would be out of the question.'

'Yes, sir, I am quite in agreement,' put in Madeleine eagerly, 'but I should like to see Cassie and Lord Kilmer, to offer them my congratulations.'

Watching from his seat beside the chess table, Sir Joseph's hawk-like eyes did not fail to notice the warm exchange of looks between his granddaughter and the newcomer.

'So you are wishing to be off gallivanting again,' he interjected harshly. 'One would think that with all the talk of war, George, it would be better for you to be at home, or in Town, in case you are needed.'

His son gave a deprecating laugh.

'Oh I don't think the Foreign Office needs my attendance quite that badly — I hold only a very junior post, you know, sir.'

'But the government is resolved for war?' asked their guest.

'It is inevitable now, I fear,' nodded Mr Sedgewick soberly. 'I was in Town on Thursday last and there was almost total unity in the House — with one or two exceptions.'

'Fox?' asked Hauxwell, producing his snuff-box.

For once Mr Sedgewick's genial manner deserted him.

'Aye, blast him,' he said bitterly. 'He could not resist the opportunity to attack Pitt — but he knows as well as any of us that we are pledged to support Holland.'

'But surely his opposition could not affect the government?' said Madeleine.

'No, of course not, but to have a division in the House, however small, on such a matter — it can only encourage the French warmongers, although in any event it is only a matter of time now.'

Mrs Sedgewick, coming in at the end of this speech, put an end to such depressing talk by saying in her gentle, practical way, 'If there must be a war, so be it. Let us therefore enjoy the peace while we may.'

'I will gladly obey that command, ma'am,' replied Mr Hauxwell. 'I hope I may be allowed the pleasure of taking you in to dinner?'

★   ★   ★

The meal was taken in almost total silence, as was usual at Stapley, and observing their guest, Miss Sedgewick supposed that Sir

Thomas had warned him before leaving Wyre of her grandfather's aversion to conversation at the table. Mr Hauxwell applied himself to his dinner with complete unconcern, but nearly overset her own gravity when he solemnly assured his host of his own dislike of idle chatter.

'In my opinion,' he remarked, 'one's faculties are much better employed upon some form of exercise — chess, for example.'

Sir Joseph's eyes lit up. 'Oh, do you play, sir — that is, do you play *well*?'

'I am considered, I believe, a formidable opponent,' replied the gentleman in an indifferent tone.

Madeleine met her mother's surprised look and rolled her eyes heavenwards. They would certainly not have the benefit of Mr Hauxwell's company now, at least until Sir Joseph had proved for himself the gentleman's ability at chess.

As she had foreseen, Madeleine had scarcely time to exchange one word with their guest after dinner before Sir Joseph called him away to the chessboard. Judging by the silence that enveloped the players, Mr Hauxwell was undoubtedly a match for her grandfather. Two hours later Sir Joseph conceded himself beaten, but any hopes the ladies might have had of conversing with their guest were dashed when he unhesitatingly accepted his host's challenge to a return game. Mr Sedgewick took himself off to the library to complete some unfinished business and the ladies were left to amuse themselves as best they could. Sir Joseph and his guest were showing no signs of ending their game when the ormulu clock on the mantel-shelf struck midnight: Madeleine could no longer conceal her fatigue and she retired to her room, more than a little discontented with the evening.

By the following morning her naturally sunny disposition had reasserted itself and she came down to breakfast in her usual good humour, even daring to tease Sir Joseph.

'I had expected you to keep to your room until noon at least, Grandpapa,' she murmured, as she saluted his wrinkled cheek.

'Away with you, saucepot,' he retorted, but mildly. 'I'm not in my dotage yet, that I cannot enjoy a late night. Though I can't remember when I last spent such a pleasant evening!'

Madeleine's eyes danced and she found her amusement mirrored in Mr Hauxwell's warm look.

'Must you return to Wyre today, sir?' she asked casually, as she selected her breakfast.

'Yes, I regret to say I must. I promised Sir

Thomas that I would return by dinnertime: I do not expect to take more than an hour and a half on the journey, so I have a reasonable time to spend here yet.' He smiled at her.

'If that's the case, sir, you can give me another game before you go,' put in Sir Joseph, laying down his fork.

'I am sorry, Father, but Hauxwell and I have already arranged to play billiards,' put in Mr Sedgewick, eyeing his parent warily for any signs of choler, but the old gentleman contented himself with a resentful glare and resumed his repast. Feeling very much like a child denied a treat, Madeleine finished her own meal in thoughtful silence, and responded absently to Mr Hauxwell's bow as he was borne away to the billiard room.

'Fine fellow,' remarked Sir Joseph, when the door had closed behind the two gentlemen. 'Where did you say he comes from?'

'Somewhere in the north — Yorkshire, I believe,' said Mrs Sedgewick. 'He is certainly most agreeable. Lady Wyre tells me he is a delightful guest.'

'Surprised she didn't snap him up for that girl of hers.'

'Cassandra is going to marry Lord Kilmer,' Madeleine told him, a little sharply.

Her grandfather's shrewd eyes regarded her.

'Aye, of course. I was forgetting that. Well, Hauxwell's a fine catch, miss. He'll do very nicely for you.'

'That is exactly what I have been thinking!' said Mrs Sedgewick, pleased to be in agreement with her father-in-law, 'He is *such* a gentleman, and rich, too, which is a great advantage. And he quite *dotes* upon Maddie.'

'That is absurd, Mama,' declared the young lady, blushing fierily. 'I really do not think you should talk in that manner.'

'Now don't start getting missish!' snapped Sir Joseph, 'You have been moping around the house ever since you returned from Wyre and it's as plain as a pikestaff you're head over heels in love with the fellow.'

'I am not!'

'Oh Maddie, do not look so outraged.' Mrs Sedgewick smiled at her. 'You are made for each other. He clearly adores you — in fact your papa and I have been expecting him to call any time this past se'ennight.'

'You are mistaken,' said Madeleine unsteadily. 'You *must* be mistaken, for he has certainly never said anything to me.'

She ran from the room and went immediately to her bedchamber, where she busied herself with the long overdue task of sorting out her wardrobe. Miss Wyre would have indulged herself in a prolonged bout of weeping to alleviate such feelings of anger and frustration as her friend was now experiencing, but Madeleine preferred activity. She was also alive to the fact that red-rimmed eyes and tear-stained cheeks did not become her and she had no intention of presenting such a pathetic picture to the world. She gained some solace from ruthlessly discarding every gown, petticoat and shawl that she had never really cared for. She had very nearly completed her task when she was summoned to the drawing-room and she went downstairs, leaving her astonished maid to take her pick from the mountain of clothes upon the bed and dispose of the rest as she thought fit.

★ ★ ★

Miss Sedgewick found her mama and Sir Joseph alone in the drawing-room, talking quietly, but they broke off their conversation as she entered.

'So there you are, my love.' Mrs Sedgewick smiled at her daughter and beckoned her forward, 'Your father and Mr Hauxwell will be here any moment. I thought you would want to bid farewell to our guest.'

'Yes, of course, Mama.'

She sat down beside Mrs Sedgewick and even as she did so the door opened to admit the two gentlemen. After a little desultory conversation Mrs Sedgewick stood up.

'I have this minute remembered a receipt for spiced beef that I promised Lady Wyre. I wonder, Mr Hauxwell, if you would be good enough to carry it to her?'

'But of course, ma'am. It would be my pleasure.'

'It will take me but a moment to find it . . . ' She hurried away, but not before she had cast a very speaking glance in Sir Joseph's direction.

'Ah yes, that reminds me,' the old gentleman struggled to his feet, leaning heavily on his stick. 'There's something I've been meaning to say to you, George. Come with me.'

'Yes, yes, sir, but Hauxwell is about to take his leave. Surely it can wait — '

'No it can't,' snapped Sir Joseph, shuffling towards the door. 'Give me your arm, man, and stop quibbling!'

Casting an apologetic look at his guest, Mr Sedgewick accompanied his father out of the room.

Madeleine remained in her seat, her eyes fixed firmly on the patterned carpet at her feet. Mr Hauxwell watched her, a slight smile, hovering about the corners of his mouth.

'I was beginning doubt that I should ever have an opportunity to speak to you.'

'Please, you need not feel obliged to say anything,' she replied, her voice barely above a whisper.

His amusement grew.

'But it is obviously expected of me.'

'Not by me, sir!' she declared, jumping up. 'It is shameless of them to put you in this position — I beg you will not say anything you might later regret!'

'You think I ought not to offer for you?' he asked her gravely.

'Yes — no — oh *pray*, don't tease me at such a time.'

'My dear girl, you are teasing yourself,' he laughed, catching her hands. 'Besides, I have not yet explained why I could not come here before now.'

'Yes,' she said, momentarily diverted, 'why *have* you kept away from us?'

'Because, my heart's darling, until yesterday I found my left arm was much too stiff to put around you — like this — and I had already decided that if I was going to ask you to marry me, I would want to be able to take you very firmly in my arms — like this.'

Emerging some minutes later from his embrace, Madeleine made no effort to free herself, but leaned against him with her cheek very comfortably nestled against his shoulder. Suddenly she looked up.

'But you have not yet asked me to marry you,' she pointed out. 'How do I know that you are in earnest?'

He let her go.

'Do you imagine,' he said awefully, 'that I would have spent the whole of last night ingratiating myself with your grandfather and this morning playing billiards with your Papa if I had *not* been in earnest?'

Madeleine's dark lashes came down to veil her laughing eyes.

'Perhaps, sir, you like chess and billiards,' she murmured provocatively.

'And perhaps you, miss, deserve a good beating.'

She ran behind a chair, half alarmed, half laughing.

'No, don't touch me, or I won't marry you!'

He held out his hand to her.

'May I take it, madam, that you have decided to honour me with your hand?'

'Yes — as long as you promise not to beat me.'

She moved into his arms and he kissed her ruthlessly.

'Unless you change your teasing ways, madam, that is one promise I cannot make.'

We do hope that you have enjoyed reading this large print book.

Did you know that all of our titles are available for purchase?

We publish a wide range of high quality large print books including:
Romances, Mysteries, Classics
General Fiction
Non Fiction and Westerns

Special interest titles available in large print are:
The Little Oxford Dictionary
Music Book
Song Book
Hymn Book
Service Book

Also available from us courtesy of Oxford University Press:
Young Readers' Dictionary
(large print edition)
Young Readers' Thesaurus
(large print edition)

For further information or a free brochure, please contact us at:
Ulverscroft Large Print Books Ltd.,
The Green, Bradgate Road, Anstey,
Leicester, LE7 7FU, England.
Tel: (00 44) **0116 236 4325**
Fax: (00 44) **0116 234 0205**

DANCE FOR A DIAMOND

Melinda Hammond

It's 1815, and Antonia Venn describes herself as a very average sort of female: a poor little dab of a girl, and certainly nothing to win the heart of a man of fortune or fashion. So in a bid for independence, and at a time when the waltz was born, she decides to open a dancing school in Bath, despite the misgivings of her family. And it is here that she takes on the beautiful Isabella Burstock as a pupil. However, this decision puts Antonia on a collision course with the young heiress's autocratic brother . . .

A LADY AT MIDNIGHT

Melinda Hammond

When Amelia Langridge accepts an invitation to stay in London as companion to Camilla Strickland, it is to enjoy herself before settling down as the wife of dependable Edmund Crannock. Camilla's intention is to capture a rich husband, and her mother is happy to allow Amelia to remain in the background. Camilla attracts the attention of Earl Rossleigh, but the earl is intent on a much more dangerous quarry, and it is Amelia who finds herself caught up in his tangled affairs . . . A merry dance through the Georgian world of duels, sparkling romance and adventure.

THE HIGHCLOUGH LADY

Melinda Hammond

Governess Verity Shore longs for a little adventure, but when Rafe Bannerman arrives to carry her off to Highclough she soon discovers that life can be a little too exciting! An estate on the edge of the wild Yorkshire Moors, Highclough is Verity's inheritance, but the land is coveted, not only by her handsome cousin Luke but also by Rafe. With her very life in danger, whom can she trust?

THE OTHER MISS FROBISHER

Ann Barker

Elfrida Frobisher leaves her country backwater and her suitor to chaperon Prudence, her eighteen-year-old niece, in London. Unfortunately, Prudence has apparently developed an attachment for an unsuitable man, which she fosters behind her aunt's back. Attempting to foil her niece's schemes and prevent a scandal, Elfrida only succeeds in finding herself involved with the eligible Rufus Tyler in a scandal of her own! Fleeing London seems the only solution — but Prudence has another plan . . . Elfrida yearns for her quiet rural existence, but it takes a mad dash in pursuit of her niece before she realises where her heart truly lies.

LADY HARTLEY'S INHERITANCE

Wendy Soliman

When Clarissa Hartley discovers her late husband's estate has been left to his illegitimate son, she fears she has lost everything. Only her godmother's son, Luc, Lord Deverill, suspects fraud. Compelled to work closely with the rakish earl, of whom she disapproves, Clarissa catches glimpses of the compassionate man lurking beneath the indolent façade. But, denying any attraction between them and ignoring his autocratic attitude, she takes matters into her own hands. Plunged into a perilous situation by dint of Clarissa's stubbornness, Luc must race against time if he is to rescue her. But can he succeed?

THE UNCONVENTIONAL MISS WALTERS

Fenella-Jane Miller

Eleanor Walters is obliged, by the terms of her aunt's will, to marry a man she dislikes: the irascible, but attractive, Lord Leo Upminster . . . Leo finds Eleanor's unconventional behaviour infuriating, her beauty irresistible and their agreement not to consummate the union increasingly impossible. It is only when he allows his frustration and jealousy to drive her away that he realizes what he has lost . . . Meanwhile, in her self-imposed exile on a neglected country estate, Eleanor becomes embroiled in riots and treachery. In a desperate race, can Leo save both her life and their marriage?